DRIFTING SNOW
An Arctic Search

For Young Readers

Tikta'liktak
Eagle Mask
The White Archer
Akavak
Wolf Run
Ghost Paddle
Whiteout

Songs of the Dream People
Kiviok's Magic Journey
Frozen Fire
River Runners
Long Claws
Black Diamonds
Ice Swords
Falcon Bow

(MARGARET K. MCELDERRY BOOKS)

For Adults

The White Dawn (a novel)
Ghost Fox (a novel)
Spirit Wrestler (a novel)
Eagle Song (a novel)
Running West (a novel)
Canadian Eskimo Art
Eskimo Prints
Ojibwa Summer
The Private Journal of Captain George F. Lyon
(edited by James Houston)

DRIFTING SNOW

SNOW

An Arctic Search

by James Houston

drawings by the author

MARGARET K. McELDERRY BOOKS · NEW YORK
Maxwell Macmillan Canada · Toronto
Maxwell Macmillan International
New York · Oxford · Singapore · Sydney

Margaret K. McElderry Books
Macmillan Publishing Company
866 Third Avenue, New York, NY 10022

Maxwell Macmillan Canada, Inc.
1200 Eglinton Avenue East, Suite 200
Don Mills, Ontario M3C 3N1

Macmillan Publishing Company is part of the
Maxwell Communication Group of Companies.

First edition   Printed in the United States of America
10 9 8 7 6 5 4 3 2 1
The text of this book is set in Caledonia.
The illustrations are rendered in pen and ink.

Library of Congress Cataloging-in-Publication Data
Houston, James A., date.
Drifting snow : an Arctic search / James Houston ; drawings by the
author. — 1st ed.   p.   cm.
Summary: Having been taken from her Arctic home when a tiny
child, a teenager returns to look for her parents and learn once
again about her Eskimo culture.
ISBN 0-689-50563-9
1. Eskimos—Juvenile fiction.   [1. Eskimos—Fiction.   2. Indians
of North America—Fiction.]   I. Title.
PZ7.H819Dr   1992   [Fic]—dc20   91-42674

ᑕᒪᑯᐊ ᐅᓂᑲᑎ ᐊᐧᐃᓇ ᑲ
ᐃᑕ ᓇ ᐊᐣᑕ ᐆᐦᐊᑕ ᑐᕝᐅᑕ ᑲ
ᐃᑲᓇ ᑐ ᐦᐊᑕ ᐊᒪᑐ ᐃᐆᐊᐸ
ᑲᐅᑕ ᒧ ᐦᐅᑕ ᐊᕒᐊᓇ ᑐ ᐊᐸ ᑕ

To
students in
the Arctic schools
and all other
students living
south of them

Author's Note

A number of years ago, some very young children had to be hurried south from their Arctic homes and parents so that their lives might be saved from tuberculosis. In the rush and confusion, the identity papers of some of those children were misplaced.

Later, these young Inuit were eager to return to the Arctic to find their families, their names, and even their own language, which they had lost. I have chosen to write about one of these young persons.

This story is based on some true events that occurred during the early part of my twelve-year stay in the eastern Arctic. Several young people undertook a determined and sometimes dangerous effort to find family roots and to understand the past.

James Houston
Cape Dorset, Baffin Island
September 1991

I

"ELIZABETH, COME SIT UP HERE WITH ME," GEORGE, the pilot, shouted. "Change places with Hugo, my engineer, who looks like he could use a catnap on our way to Nesak Island."

Hugo left the copilot's seat and crawled back into the body of the single-engine plane. Elizabeth Queen eased out of her seat and moved forward to sit beside the pilot, George Charity, who was an old friend. The only other passengers were an Inuit woman, Nepeesha, and her small son.

Elizabeth fastened her seat belt and looked at the plane's dashboard, covered with radio compasses, switches, dials, and gauges, then out through the curving front windshield and side windows of the small, rugged plane.

"Wonderfully clear blue day up here," said George, "now that we're above that morning blanket of Arctic fog."

"I love flying," said Elizabeth, "especially in this plane with you. And who knows, maybe we're flying over the very place where I was born."

"That's what we're here for. That's what we're trying to discover," George answered cheerfully. "It's my guess that you were born somewhere here in the eastern or central Arctic. I hope this small island of Nesak off the Baffin Island coast will prove to be the very place we've been searching for."

"Oh, I hope so, too," said Elizabeth. But the truth was, she was slowly losing hope that she would ever find her family or her home.

"Tell me again how old you were when you left your family," George said to her.

"I don't really know, but I guess I must have been about two."

"Judging by my own daughter," George told her, "you look to me to be about thirteen or maybe fourteen."

"That's what the nurses and my teachers guess. That's about the age I feel I am, and that matches with my grade in school."

George nodded. "I've heard of other Arctic kids who were misplaced like you. Their identification papers had been mixed up on the icebreaker before it sailed south to take them out to hospital. I mean, maybe the ship's crewmen were the ones who lost your papers and your name tag."

Elizabeth moved her head closer to the pilot's because of the roaring engine noise. "It might have happened that way. I've heard that seven or eight other kids had their identities lost like me. At least four of those have found their families now."

"Don't worry," said George, "we'll find yours. See that cove there?" He tipped the plane's wing down and pointed. "See the small boat propped up in the snow on the shore with half a dozen winter tents behind it? That camp's called Akiaktolaolavik." He looked at the plane's dials and then his wristwatch. "It means we're more than halfway to Nesak. Believe me, it's a lot easier flying in the springtime here, when the hours of daylight are getting longer. I dread feeling my way through December's icy gloom."

"I'll bet it's cold, too." Elizabeth shivered.

"What if you do find your family living here on Nesak Island?" George asked her. "What are you going to do?"

"I don't know," Elizabeth answered. "I've been dreaming of finding them for so long that now I'm almost *afraid* to find them. Almost afraid to have to decide."

"See way up there ahead of us?" George nodded. "That soft blue hump shaped like a hat? That's Nesak Island. I hope that's the very place that will turn out to be your home."

Elizabeth stared in silence at the hazy island standing alone in the partly frozen sea.

"You'd better go back to your own seat now," the pilot said. "Send Hugo up to help me."

Elizabeth changed seats with Hugo and felt the small plane shudder as George lowered the wing flaps and started down. She smiled at Nepeesha and the small boy in her lap, then fastened her seat belt. She crossed her fingers inside her mitts and closed her eyes. Yes, this could be the very island where her family lived, the place she had been dreaming of for almost all her life.

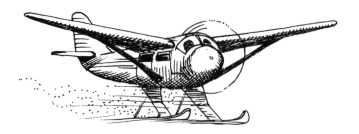

II

POOTA WAS THE FIRST TO HEAR THE DISTANT DRON-
ing of the plane. He shook his sister awake. "Uvilu,
listen. Do you hear it?" he asked, then wriggled out
of his sleeping bag and opened the small wooden door
of his family's double-walled winter tent. "I can see
it," he told her. "It's coming down straight toward our
island."

The plane seemed to slide down through the ice-
cold morning sky, looking at first no bigger than a blue
meat fly. Poota pulled on his new sealskin boots, then
went back to the door. He watched the pilot tip the
plane's wing and begin to circle low, searching the
hard-packed ice of the fjord for the best place to land.
Poota knew the pilot was trying to judge the wind's
direction by watching gusts from the silver drifts of
snow that scurried across the surface of the frozen sea.
There was no landing strip on Nesak, a rough, rocky

island named with the Inuit word meaning 'hat' because the island was shaped just like a hat.

The four families dwelling above the beach continued to live their nomadic lives in spite of modern times. They moved with every season, following the animals—birds, fish, and caribou—animals that supported them and allowed them to stay alive. In winter and in early spring, these hunting families lived on this island. Later, they would pull their boats on sleds behind their snowmobiles across the great expanse of sea ice to the mouth of the Kokjuak River on Baffin Island. It would be a long day's journey for them, but the plane had taken only a few minutes to cross.

Inside their winter tent, Poota pulled on his silver-spotted, knee-length, outer sealskin pants, and then his best navy-blue parka with red-and-white braid near his hips and around his wrists. Setting his many-colored woolen hat upon his head, then pulling up his hood, he hurried through the tent's low door. Any day when they had visitors was a very special day.

As the strong metal skis of the bright red plane touched down on the snow, he watched the plane bounce, then hop, then skim roughly over the hard white drifts.

Kiawak, Poota's father, hurried out close behind him. Together they rolled their long sled over onto its runners and, attaching two dog lines, pulled it toward the plane, which had now turned and was sliding toward them, its propeller a sheen of silver in the morning light.

The plane slid to a stop and Hugo, the engineer, jumped out. He pulled up his hood against the cold, and moved back along the plane's side to open the rear door. He held up one hand in its big, sub-Arctic, Indian-beaded mitt to help the passengers jump down.

Poota knew both George and Hugo. They were the ones who did most of the flying in this part of the country.

"Hi, Kiawak. Hi, Poota," the pilot called, as he climbed out the front door of the plane. He was a man about Kiawak's age, broad-shouldered, with steel-rimmed glasses and a thick mustache turning gray. "How's life going around here?"

Poota smiled at him, his bright teeth flashing in his sun-browned face. "Going good, George," he answered. "How about you two?"

Poota watched as a girl hopped down from the plane's rear door onto the hard-packed drift. She was Inuk. She wore an orange-and-yellow scarf around her neck and a light-blue nylon parka with no fur trim on the hood. Her hair was blue-black and shiny, woven into two old-fashioned braids. She looked pale to Poota, not like the girls he knew, whose faces were deeply tanned from the spring sun.

Behind the girl, Hugo helped Nepeesha to climb down carefully. She was carrying her small son, Noah, who had been very ill. Now he was well again. They were returning to their family from a hospital in the south. Nepeesha shook hands with Poota and his father. She was Tudlik's wife, whom they had known and traveled with all their lives.

The pilot introduced Elizabeth. "This newcomer is Elizabeth Queen," he said.

It was a strange name for a girl, thought Poota, a girl with almond-shaped eyes and a smooth, attractive Inuk face. He and his father shook hands with her, then helped Hugo unload the plane's few bags and packages onto their sled.

Elizabeth smiled at Poota. "Do you live here all the time?" she asked him while they walked beside Nepeesha and small Noah up toward the four large tents, which were half buried in snow.

"No," Poota answered her, using his own language of Inuktitut. "We move around to different places, hunting, fishing, living off the land."

There was a pause. Elizabeth shivered in the icy wind, then said, "I understand almost nothing of what you have just said."

"You're Inuk, aren't you?" Poota asked in English, looking steadily at her.

"Yes, I'm Inuk, if that's what being an Inuit means, but I don't really know my own language. I was separated from my family. I grew up in a Canadian hospital in the south, mostly with Ojibwa and Cree Indians. Does anyone here speak Ojibwa, Cree, or French? I speak a bit of those languages. But I guess that's not going to help me here. I'm not even sure what Inuk means. Is that like Inuit or Eskimo?"

"Yes," said Poota. "We've got a lot to talk about, but I've got to help now."

Fifteen other people from Nesak Island were now clustered to welcome the plane's crew and passengers. Tudlik, Nepeesha's husband, smiled and greeted his wife and child, then shook hands with Elizabeth before he gathered his young son into his arms. Together, he and Nepeesha hurried off toward their tent.

"This Inuk girl, her name's Elizapee," Poota told the others crowded close around them.

Each of them pulled off a mitt to shake her hand, as well as the hands of the two flying men. *"Kano-wepeet,"* they greeted her.

Elizabeth smiled and answered them, *"Nakomik!* All I know how to say to you is 'thank you.' "

Poota could see that she was turning her back to the wind and shuddering. "This is my sister, Uvilu," he told her in English. "She will take you into our family's tent. You go in and have some tea. I'll stay here with my dad and help with the freight."

"Thanks." After a moment's hesitation, she added, "My name is Eliza*beth*, not Eliza*pee!"* Then she ran after Uvilu.

The tent was lit by two seal-oil-burning stone lamps and a hissing pressure lantern. Its outside walls were insulated by neatly cut and piled snow blocks. Poota and George and Hugo came into the tent a few minutes later, loaded with packages and two blue canvas bags. Packed in them were engine parts, a fishnet, rifle cartridges, and a small hand-operated sewing machine.

Elizabeth Queen sat next to Poota's mother, Maylee, on the wide, low bed that stretched across the whole back of the tent. People from the other tents crowded in. Poota's grandfather, Paar, who always enjoyed guests, sat at the far end of the bed, smiling at Elizabeth. Everyone, young and old, was trying to talk to her in Inuktitut and laughing in disbelief that she, an Inuk, could not answer them and understood almost nothing of what they said.

"Help me," Elizabeth called out to Poota. "Help me, please. Tell them I'm sorry I cannot speak my own language."

"*Inuktitut kauyimangitok,*" Poota said to his family, and there was silence.

Then everyone started talking at once.

"They want to know where you come from. Where does your family live? I've already told them your name is Elizapee," Poota translated, forgetting what Elizabeth had said about her name.

"I don't know." Elizabeth sighed, for it seemed to her that no one else in this house spoke English. "I've looked so hard for my home and family. Lots of people guessed my parents might be living in this camp with you."

There was another silence, with only the harsh sound of the wind slapping against the roof of the tent.

"Did any of your people ever lose a young child, almost a baby? Did any of you lose a little girl?" Elizabeth asked.

After Poota translated her words, Kiawak asked him, "Does she remember her father's name? Her mother's name?"

Poota interpreted his question to Elizabeth Queen.

She looked down at her tea mug. "I don't know my father's or my mother's name, or where I lived, or if I had any brothers or sisters. I'm not even sure how old I am."

"Tell us every early thing you can remember," Poota said.

Elizabeth began to speak hesitantly. "The first, the earliest thing that I remember, is the ship. I remember that I was riding warmly in my mother's hood when the ship arrived. When it came close, it looked so huge I was afraid. No wonder, for I was probably not yet three years old. I can remember a boy, perhaps an older brother of mine, maybe he was six or seven. He kept running up and down the beach yelling, '*Oomi-jack, oomi-jack.*' "

"Wait, wait!" Poota held up his hand. "You must be trying to say *umiakjuak*. That's our word for a large ship. You haven't forgotten all your Inuktitut."

Elizabeth went on. "That image of the ship is still strong in my mind. It was red near the water, then gray, with dozens of round black eyes and fluttering flags and steam coming out the top."

Elizabeth remembered when the ship's horn began to hoot and its loud bells clanged and nothing more until she was carried up a ladder, still in her mother's hood, from a loading barge to the ship's deck. Then she was in a room with other people while glaring lights seemed brighter than the sun. She started crying when her mother lifted her out of her parka and handed her to a stranger dressed in white. Then another person came and they carried her along a frightening passage, moving far away from her mother. She began to cry harder, then to scream when white lights flashed at her. After doing other terrifying things, the person in white placed her once more in the safety of her mother's hood. The noisy iron barge carried them back to shore.

"Oh, I remember it felt good to be safe once more inside our tent," Elizabeth told Poota, "to feel the heat of my mother's back and watch my father making funny faces for me and to hear other children playing close around me.

"It was on the following day, perhaps, that two strange people came into our tent. They were dressed in white but wore raincoats over their shoulders and rain hats on their heads. They had an Inuk who could speak to my mother and father for them. Those in white made marks on paper. Soon I could hear my mother sobbing and feel her shoulders shaking, and then the strong voice of my father talking strangely. Everyone walked out of the tent together into the rain and down onto the edge of the beach. I peeked out over the edge of my mother's parka and saw the barge nearby and the frightening ship casting light across the darkening water.

"One of the two people in white reached inside my mother's parka," Elizabeth said, "and lifted me out and wrapped a blanket around me. When I saw the terrified looks on the faces of my mother and father, I began to cry, to scream, but my family could only let the tears run down their cheeks. They could not follow me as I was carried away."

Elizabeth went on. "I do not remember anything else until I was taken off the ship. Then I could smell and see huge green trees and, like the other children, I was put into something on round wheels that rolled over the land and in this way we were taken to the hospital. It was a frightening place at first, full of strange, sharp smells, more people dressed in white or blue with hats, who always gave good smiles to me. But I was only looking for my real mother, my father, and the children I had always known.

"I stayed south in that hospital for more than three years, then in a boarding school for seven years. I was befriended by a family in that city, and they were like relatives to me. I didn't know for a long time that someone had lost my papers and my identification tag. The first language I spoke was English, then French, and some Cree and Ojibwa, which I learned from the nurses, other children, and my teachers in the Indian hospital school.

"I don't know how old I am, but I must be about thirteen, or maybe fourteen. I thought my real name was Elizabeth Queen, but a teacher told me later that it was only a made-up name. Because the picture of Queen Elizabeth of England was on the paper money they used, they had decided to name me Elizabeth Queen."

No one spoke inside the tent after Poota had interpreted her words.

"So"—Elizabeth tried to smile—"I don't know who I am, or where I came from. I've got to find out more about myself, my place, my people."

"You're you," said Poota, "that's all you really need to know."

George now spoke to Poota. "This is the fifth Inuit camp we've visited, as well as almost every small settlement in the eastern Arctic. The government in the south chartered me to fly Elizabeth up here and asked me to act as kind of a guardian to her, to give her a chance to search for her family. Are you certain no one here remembers anyone losing a child?"

Poota's mother and the other men and women looked sad when Poota translated.

"No," they had to answer.

"*Nakomik*, thank you for trying to help me," Elizabeth said. "Thank you for the tea and bannock. Thank you, Poota, for interpreting for me."

"I'm sorry to say this," George told Poota, looking at his watch, "but we've got to be going now. The wind is getting stronger. We're going to take on gas at Cape Dorset, then hurry to make it back to Igaluit in Frobisher Bay tonight."

The pilot turned to Poota's father. "Here's an envelope for you. There is money in it for those last two boxes of carvings you gave me to take to the cooperative. And here's another envelope for Tudlik." He also gave envelopes to Kakak and Pudlo, two men from the other tents. "You all made good money this time."

Poota translated quickly.

"My father says thanks," said Poota, "but there's nothing here for us to buy with money."

"Later, later!" George laughed. "You'll probably be coming into the settlement before next winter."

"We certainly will," said Poota. "My mother says we'll need a lot of things by then."

"The good time for carving outside is coming now

because the weather's turning warm," said Kiawak. "It's almost spring."

"Stay well," said George to all of them. "Good seeing you again. Nice talking to you, Poota. Thanks for being the interpreter."

"I'm glad to help you," Poota said. Then he looked very seriously at Elizabeth. "Do you really want to go? I mean, are you ready to go?"

"I don't want to go," said Elizabeth Queen. After a moment's pause, she continued softly, but with determination. "I'd like to stay right here on this island with all of you. You're such kind people. I've got to belong somewhere. Would your family and the others in this camp let me stay?"

Uvilu offered her more tea and whispered shyly in English, "I hope you stay." So Poota wasn't the only one who spoke English. Elizabeth was relieved.

George looked serious and said to Elizabeth, "Do you mean that? Do you really want to stay?"

"Yes, I do," Elizabeth answered. She then asked Poota, "What do you think?"

"Stay," said Poota impulsively. "I hope you'll stay."

"Then ask your family, and the others in this camp, if she can stay here," said George. "I'm responsible for Elizabeth Queen. I've got to look out for her."

Poota spoke. "Elizabeth says she wants to stay here for a while to live with us." He translated to his family and those from the other tents what Elizabeth and George had said.

A girl standing just inside the tent's small door said

in English, "We don't like strangers coming to stay in our camp."

Others stared more closely at Elizabeth Queen's pale face. Poota held his breath, waiting for the answer that the elders in the camp would give, fearful that they might decide to send her away.

III

ELIZABETH WAITED, SHIVERING A LITTLE FROM NER-
vousness and from the Arctic cold that had gathered
inside the winter tent, because Sharni, the daughter
of Nepeesha and Tudlik, was standing at the door and
holding it half open. She seemed eager to hear the
elders tell Elizabeth to leave.

Poota's mother and father spoke seriously together,
sometimes glancing at Elizabeth and at the others
around them before continuing. There was a long silence in the tent, then the grandfather coughed in the
cold and called something out to Poota's parents.

Kiawak spoke to Poota using words that seemed to
come from deep inside his throat, his lips scarcely
moving as he formed each sound. Then they all talked
together.

Poota listened very carefully before he turned his
head and looked straight at Elizabeth.

"My parents and my grandfather and my sister, Uvilu, all say yes. They will be glad to have you join us, and the other parents agree."

"Oh, please thank them," Elizabeth answered. "I'll do my share of work. I'll try to learn from everyone in the best way I can."

When Poota interpreted Elizabeth's words, the grandfather spoke again and Poota added, "He says we all welcome you."

Elizabeth smiled at them. "Most of all, I want you to teach me my own language and Inuit ways."

Elizabeth heard the small wooden door slam closed. Sharni, the only one who had spoken against her, was gone.

"Tell her," Poota's mother, Maylee, said, "that it's difficult for us to say her name in our language. It sounds strange. We like to say Elizapee. That sounds softer, better to our ears."

"Then my name shall be Elizapee, *Ee-liz-a-pee.*"

George smiled, "Good luck, Elizapee. I have known Kiawak's family for a very long time, and I'm sure they'll take good care of you. I'll drop down to see you next time I'm hired to fly this way. I'll send word to your nurses and the teachers that you've found a good home for now, here among friends. Poota, why don't you come down to the plane and bring back Elizabeth's backpack and sleeping bag?"

The other families began to leave. George ducked through the low door. Passing the dark granite rocks blown clear of snow, he hurried across the beach.

The red plane started with a cold chug and then a

rising roar. Turning into the wind, it ran over the hardened drifts until it soared into the air. George circled the camp once, waved, then sped away toward the dim sunset, half hidden by drifting curtains of fine snow.

Inside the tent, Poota's mother and Uvilu increased the flow of seal oil into long even flames in their stone lamp.

Elizapee soon discovered that Poota's sister, Uvilu, who seemed about her own age, spoke more than a little English. "After all," Uvilu said, "I'm still attending school."

"School?" said Elizapee. "Is there a school around here?"

"Not an ordinary school. We've got a special kind of school right in here," said Poota proudly, pointing at their tent floor.

"Where?" Elizapee asked.

"Well, there's no real schoolhouse. Tomasi, he's our teacher. He just gathers us together and uses one of these four tents to do his teaching. He's an Inuk, maybe about twenty-one years old. He knows a lot about education. He went outside, to the south, to teacher's college. You'll like him."

"Where is he now?" Elizapee asked.

Uvilu explained, "He's gone on his snowmobile over to one of the two camps on the mainland where he also teaches. Our school is called an itinerant school because it lets us move with our families, so we can live the way we've always lived."

Poota, who had come back into the tent, smiled at

Elizapee as he put down her backpack and sleeping bag. "When you see Tomasi, you tell him what grade you're in, and he'll be glad to teach you, too."

"It sounds good to me!" said Elizapee.

"It is," said Poota. "My dad and mom, and especially my grandfather, they don't like the bigger settlements. This is an experiment. With a teacher traveling around sometimes with us, we can all live free, the way we want to. That's how they teach some classes over in Greenland. You'll have a chance to try it yourself."

"*Eekee!* It's cold." Uvilu shuddered.

Elizapee nodded and said, "*Eekee!*" She was pleased to be using a real word in Inuktitut. The very word felt good to her as her warm breath forced it from between her lips and turned it into two short bursts of steam. It was a word she would remember, a word that now belonged to her.

From her backpack, Elizapee took out a large chocolate bar and her small pocket knife. Using it, she divided the chocolate evenly and gave the pieces to every member of the family and one to herself. It had been an exciting day for all of them. Elizapee went to sleep quickly that night somewhere near the warm middle of the wide family bed.

"The wind has gone," said Poota in the morning. "I'm going hunting with my father. We'll be back tonight or maybe tomorrow. It doesn't matter which," he explained to Elizapee. "It's not going to get really dark anymore, now that winter's gone and spring is almost here. Uvilu says that she will be glad to help you."

Poota and Kiawak drank mugs of tea and ate some meat and bannock, then, carrying extra wind pants and parkas, they left the tent with their hunting bags, harpoons, and rifles in canvas cases.

Soon Elizapee and the women could hear the whine of the snowmobiles as Kiawak and Poota, with the other hunters, headed around the island toward the breaking Arctic ice that lay beyond.

Uvilu bent forward and looked at Elizapee, then pointed at her mother. "My *annana*, 'mother,'" she said, pronouncing the Inuktitut word very slowly. "Her name is Maylee." Then she pointed to the far side of the wide bed and said, "*Atatachiak*, 'my grandfather.' His name is Paar. It means 'entrance to the igloo.'"

Elizapee repeated their names very carefully.

"My mother says you should always sleep same place, okay? With your head toward the door as we do." Uvilu pulled her sleeping bag toward herself and pushed the blankets of her younger brother, Emik, over to make more room on the wide bed for Elizapee.

"Sure, it's okay." Elizapee busied herself rolling up her sleeping bag, then sat on top of it.

"Your blue parka's very pretty, but no good up here," said Uvilu. "You'll soon get *eekee*—cold—in it!"

Maylee got up and hung a soft, warm caribou skin over Elizapee's shoulders. Then, from the back of the tent, Maylee brought forward a large roll, which she unwrapped very carefully until yards and yards of thick white woolen duffel lay on the bed.

"*Okoyuk*, 'warm,' " said Uvilu, and Elizapee repeated *okoyuk*, the word for 'warm,' as she felt the new material.

Looking carefully at Elizapee, but not measuring her, Maylee began to plan and cut a new parka. She cut the parka in the style all young unmarried women wore, with a slightly wider fur-trimmed hood and much more stylish sleeves, and without the long tail and child-carrying pouch that married women wore.

Elizapee helped and was surprised at how quickly the three of them, working together, were able to sew the body of the new parka. With sinew, they carefully hand-sewed a beautiful white fur trim around the hood and smaller ruffs around the wrists and at the bottom. As evening came, Maylee brought out her loon-skin sewing bag and unrolled lengths of finger-wide, colored woolen braid. Maylee offered Elizapee her choice of the colors that she had, then using her new hand-operated sewing machine, she sewed the bright braid on the white sailcloth parka cover they had also made for Elizapee. Elizapee had chosen stripes of orange and yellow to go around the wrists and near the bottom.

At last, it was time to try on both the parka and its cover. Elizapee missed being able to see herself in a full-length mirror, but she felt warm and comfortable inside the perfect-fitting garments.

"Thank you," she said to all of them. "*Nakomik.*"

"*Elali,*" Uvilu answered. "That means 'you're welcome.'"

Elizapee repeated, "*Nakomik, nakomik,*" and then she got her diary and a pencil from her backpack and wrote down all the words that she had learned that day.

Eager to try out her new parka, Elizapee went outside with Uvilu. Her whole body felt warm. Only her feet could still feel the cold. The girls watched the clouds turn fiery red in the west, and Jupiter, the first star, sparkled down to them like a bright ice chip in the cold blue evening sky.

Elizapee did not eat seal meat with the others in the tent that night. It was raw. But she had hot tea and some red jam on a large square pilot biscuit, which tasted good but was so hard that she had to dip it in the tea before she could bite it.

Maylee went outside the tent and peered at the frozen sea. The day was done, but the hunters had not returned.

Elizapee removed her leather snow boots and outer clothing, then slipped into her sleeping bag, lying comfortably between Uvilu and her younger brother, who was already sound asleep.

Elizapee looked at the wristwatch her favorite teacher had given her and thought of the TV program she would be watching if she were still living in the city. She would try to forget all that while she was living here with this new family she had found. This was what she had longed for. She thought of Poota and wondered if he was freezing cold away on the sea ice in this bitter weather. Would the men stay out until morning, or would they come back while she was asleep?

Next morning when she awoke, neither Kiawak nor Poota nor any of the other hunters had returned. Where were they? What had happened to them?

IV

LATE THAT MORNING, POOTA, HIS FATHER, AND THE rest of the hunters came staggering toward the camp, exhausted.

"Where are the snowmobiles?" Elizapee asked Uvilu.

"We don't know," Uvilu answered. "Maybe they're lost, but we're grateful to see all our men coming home again! They're safe!"

The hunters were so tired they moved very slowly as they walked up to the tents.

None of the women, not even the children, called out, "What happened to the snowmobile?" as they would certainly have done in the southern places where Elizabeth Queen had lived. Instead, they went quietly inside with the men and poured out mugs of hot sugared tea and fed them some rich meat stew.

After a while, Uvilu's father, Kiawak, spoke in a sad

voice, "We lost all three snowmobiles. The ice broke off and they went adrift on the moving floes."

Poota couldn't even look at Elizapee as he translated those sad words to her.

"It was no one's fault," Kiawak went on. "We saw some seals along the floe edge and did not wish to take the snowmobiles and their engine noise with us. Instead, we walked quietly toward them. But the seals disappeared in the moving ice. We waited awhile, then turned and started back.

"Soon we could see that a large piece of ice had been broken off the main floe by the tide and it was moving out, carrying all three of our snowmobiles away. Poota and Pudlo's son, Ipelle, ran very fast, but the gap in the ice was already much too wide for them to jump across. All of us had to stand there and watch our three best snowmobiles drift away. Now we only have one old snowmobile left."

"*Ayurnamat*," said Poota's mother.

"*Ayurnamat*," said Uvilu.

"What does that mean?" whispered Elizapee to Poota, who had sat down near her.

"*Ayurnamat* means 'it can't be helped.' Can't be changed. The snowmobiles are gone."

Poota was so tired and discouraged that he held his head in his hands. "We'll eat and sleep for a while, then go up on top of this island's hat and have a look with the bring-near glass this afternoon when the light is best. My father says maybe the ice carrying the snowmobiles will have been caught by other pieces of ice and we might take the old snowmobile and find a path to them farther down the coast."

Elizapee, like the other women, said no more. A hunter's life was hard and there was nothing any of them could do. Families used snowmobiles now instead of dogsleds as their best means of getting around. Dog teams had become a thing of the past. The Kiawak family kept only one young bitch, Lao, to warn them against bears.

When Elizapee came back from taking a walk with Uvilu, the men had already gone onto the ice again. Uvilu said they would be searching along its edges, hoping they might find the missing snowmobiles.

Two days and nights passed before the men returned. Once more they came staggering in dead tired, all of them hungry as wolves.

"Now this camp only has one battered old snowmobile to share among four families," Poota told Elizapee. "That is barely enough to take us anywhere. Still, we'll do the best we can."

During that first spring moon, the winds and ice were bad for hunting, and they had almost no food left in the camp.

When Elizapee awoke one morning, the men and all their hunting gear were gone. She rose and went outside with Uvilu. On that day neither of them took even one bite of the family's dwindling supply of food.

The spring brightness was so great outside, because of the sun's rays bouncing off the snow, that the two girls hurried back inside the tent and put on their dark glasses. Lao followed them as they went down to look at the new barrier ice that had been heaved ashore by the full moon's tide. Elizapee could see four girls about their own age there with two small children. The girls

stood in a circle and seemed to be preparing themselves for something special.

Elizapee recognized the girl named Sharni. She was
no taller than the rest, but she held herself very
straight, and her parka seemed a brighter white and
better fitting, with more decorative bands of braid,
than the others'. Her sealskin boots were sleek and
black, rising smoothly to her knees.

Three of the girls nodded to Elizapee and Noah
came and clutched her leg. But Sharni turned her
head away, not even looking at Elizapee. Sharni's dark
glasses covered her eyes, but her unsmiling lips re-
vealed her feelings.

The other girls invited Elizapee and Uvilu to join
in the bird hunt they were planning. When they joined
the group, Sharni turned, and, followed by the two
children, walked away from all of them. The others
watched her go.

"It's me," Elizapee said sadly to her new friends.
"Sharni doesn't like me."

They looked at their feet.

"It's not you." Nuna spoke in unsure English. "It's
Poota. Sharni wants him. Yes. Two winters past, she
lost her *uingasak* out on the moving ice."

"What's an *uingasak*?" Elizapee asked.

"He's meant to be a husband sometime later, the
boy your family picks to become your husband when
you grow old enough to have one."

"Oh," Elizapee said. "I've never heard of that."

"Don't families do that where you come from?"
Nuna asked.

"I don't think so," Elizapee admitted. "I never heard of it."

"They do it here," Uvilu told her. "Poota, he had a young girl he was supposed to marry when he got old enough to need a wife. It was arranged by my father and mother with another good hunter and his wife. This was long ago, when Poota was only two winters old."

"That sounds kind of young," Elizapee said.

"Well, it's never going to happen now." Uvilu looked unhappy. "That girl had to move away with her whole family. They live far west of here." She pointed. "A place called Tuktoyaktok. That girl's father got a good job working in the western Arctic."

Uvilu shaded her eyes. "Sharni hopes our family and her family will decide that it's okay if she and Poota get married."

"Does he want to marry her?" Elizapee asked.

The other girls hunched their shoulders and smiled. "*Kauyimangilunga,*" they each answered, saying they didn't know.

Nuna said, "We think that Poota is starting to really like you, Elizapee. That's the reason Sharni goes away when you come near."

"I can't help that." Elizapee shook her head. "I'm glad he likes me, but I wish we could all be friends. What could I do to become Sharni's friend?"

The others shrugged their shoulders. Then, gathering their bird-throwing sticks, they set off in single file, walking so smoothly and easily over the hard, rough snowdrifts that Elizapee could scarcely keep up with them.

During their long hunt, they saw only nine ptarmigan, all of them in one flock that quickly flew away, their white feathers hiding them against the snow. The girls had climbed the highest peak on Nesak Island and from there had looked out to the distant floe edge, where the ice had broken away and drifted eastward, leaving an immense, dark, open body of seawater. Uvilu pointed out half a dozen dots that were their hunting men, waiting and hoping for the seals to come. But not once that day did they hear the sound of a rifle fired.

How can this go on? Elizapee thought. If Kiawak and Poota and the other hunters find no food—she felt her stomach clutch with hunger.

She looked at her watch. It was almost six o'clock. What wouldn't she give right now, she thought, to be sitting down at a table with the family she had lived with in the city, the ones who had been so kind to her before she started on this desperate Arctic search to find her parents. She remembered their last dinner together. They had taken her to a wonderful restaurant. The tall waiter had handed her a large menu card. She had chosen shrimp salad for her appetizer and creamed breast of chicken and sweet potatoes as her main course, followed by a huge slice of chocolate cake for dessert. Her knees grew weak as she thought about that meal, about the abundance of city food, so easily ordered and quickly served. Now her stomach pinched again and she knew for the first time the bitter taste of hunger in her mouth.

The girls followed Uvilu down off Nesak Hill. On

the beach, they saw Sharni walking by herself. She did not look up at them, but stopped to examine something in the upheaval of ice and snow. When Uvilu and the others reached her, Elizapee and Lao still trailed behind a bit. Sharni pointed to a crack in the snow and ice and spoke to the others in rapid Inuktitut.

Uvilu came closer to Elizapee. "Sharni says the full moon last night made the shore ice rise then break, and the low tide has pulled the water far out to sea."

They followed Sharni along the edge of the crack until they came to a diamond-shaped opening in the ice. It's smaller than the top of a school desk, Elizapee thought. When she looked down, she could feel a sense of dizziness and fear rise up in her. The under-edges of the gaping crack were made of blue-green ice that seemed to be shaped like a monster's jaws, with sharp icicles for teeth dripping down into the freezing darkness below.

Sharni spoke quickly and Uvilu translated, "Sharni asks you, Elizapee, if you're afraid to go down through that crack with her."

V

ELIZAPEE STARED AT SHARNI IN TERROR AND AT FIRST she could not answer.

"It shouldn't frighten you too much," said Sharni, wrinkling her nose. "Look! Can you see the sand and icy stones and slippery seaweed down there?"

"Yes, I can see them," Elizapee almost whispered. "They seem a long way down to me."

"*Kapiashukpeet?*" Sharni asked her.

When Elizapee could not answer, Sharni smiled at her, not in a friendly way.

Uvilu said, "She's asking you again if you're afraid."

Elizapee answered finally, "No, I am not afraid."

Uvilu said, "See, she is not afraid to go down the crack."

"Why would anyone go down inside that crack?" Elizapee asked.

"For *ushuks*, clams. We've got to have them. Our

families have no food at all. The wind is wrong for sealing, and I believe our hunters will come back again with nothing."

"I'm going down," said Sharni. "Uvilu, will you help me climb down?"

"Yes, I will," said Uvilu. "Elizapee, will you take her other wrist?"

"No," said Sharni. "She's too weak. She doesn't know how. Nuna, you help me."

So Nuna took her wrist. Together, she and Uvilu carefully lowered Sharni down the crack. Then, when Sharni told them to, they let her drop.

"Namuktok," they heard her call up to them.

"She's telling us there's enough room between the sea bottom and the ice above her to bend and crawl," Uvilu told Elizapee. "She's found two clams already. She says, *'Pingashut, sitamut,* three, four. . . .' She's counting. She's found more big ones. You help me, Elizapee, hold my wrist. I'm going down. Nuna will hold my other wrist."

In a moment, Uvilu had disappeared beneath the ice.

"I'm coming, too," Elizapee called to her. "How am I going to get down?"

"Are you sure you want to come down here?" Uvilu called up.

"Yes," said Elizapee. "I'm coming."

"Nuna will hold your wrists and help you down. I'll try to catch your legs."

Elizapee and Nuna clasped tight to each other's wrists, then kneeling, straining, Nuna let Elizapee carefully down. Uvilu caught her around the knees and lowered her into the dripping gloom.

Sharni had already disappeared somewhere beneath the ice. Looking up, Elizapee thought of a dusty gray windowpane, a pane that was as thick as she was tall. They heard Sharni's voice echoing dully somewhere far away in front of them.

"She says, '*Avatit*,' twenty. There are many more clams where she is." Uvilu bent low and the two girls tried to follow the sound of Sharni's voice.

"I hate it down here"—Elizapee shivered—"with this huge weight of dripping ice above me." She could feel her new parka rubbing against the ice. As the wet, gray space grew lower and narrower, she had to move on her hands and knees.

"*Tika! Tika!*" called Uvilu. "Look at them! Clams everywhere. Gather them, pick them out quickly. Don't try to clean them off. Get every one you see!"

"Where am I going to put them?" Elizapee cried to Uvilu, who now seemed no bigger than the shadow of a crawling baby.

"Fill the hood of your parka. Stuff your pockets with them. Tie your parka at the bottom with your scarf and fill it like a sack. Gather every clam you can."

"Oh, my good new parka," Elizapee moaned. But remembering the hunger of the families and the rich taste of clams, she did as she was told.

Elizapee guessed she must have gathered perhaps a hundred of the big, gritty long-necked clams, using her new parka like a bag around herself, when suddenly she heard a long huff like some icy giant giving off a dreadful, moaning sigh.

"*Ajii*, yahh!" yelled Uvilu. "It's the ice. Sharni, come back, come back! It's breaking, Sharni! The ice is falling in on us."

Some distance forward, Elizapee could hear Sharni give a terrified scream. Then the giant sighing sound came rushing past her again, just above her head, and looking up, Elizapee could see the thick gray ice cracking, breaking into a thousand bright white streaks, flashing like lightning as it shattered and caved in, dropping an unbelievable weight of ice just to the right of her.

She fell on her belly and screamed for Uvilu, for Sharni, for Nuna. But no one answered her in the dripping silence.

The heavy ceiling of ice just above Elizapee continued to moan and groan and sometimes snap, throwing showers of freezing chips and water spraying down upon her.

This whole ice ceiling is collapsing, she thought. I'll never get out of this place alive. She wanted to jerk her scarf from around her hips and let the whole load of clams fall out so that she could be slim and scramble catlike to the only faint spot of light that she could see.

Then, without warning, the lightninglike shattering and cracking started again, to her left this time, and she could feel the giant huff of air as more of the massive roof collapsed, dropping another huge fall of ice around her. Now Elizapee's passage back to the diamond-shaped hole of light had disappeared, and there were only dark shadows around her. She screamed, then screamed again. But there was no one who could hear her. The dangerous moaning of the dripping ice grew loud again as the sound came closer to her.

Elizapee crouched in terror, looking up at the maze of cracked lines above her head that were spreading like shattered windshield glass. Then, faintly from above, she could hear the voice of Nuna calling, calling, using each one of their names.

"Uvilooo . . . Sharniii . . . Elizapeee!"

She heard no answers from the other two.

Elizapee was almost afraid to yell back her answer, fearing that the very sound might shatter the cracked ceiling and cause it to fall on her. But she could not stay where she was like a frightened rabbit in an ice hole, with the hard, cold clams packed like stones around her body.

"Nunaaa! Nunaaa!" she yelled. "It's me, Elizapee! Can you hear me?"

Elizapee could hear the crunching sound of running feet as Nuna rushed over the snow-covered ice toward the place where she lay.

"Elizapee . . . was that you? Call again! Where are you?"

"I'm here, down here. Not far below you now," Elizapee cried. "Be careful. Don't collapse the ice."

Elizapee waited, shivering in the ghostly shadows. She could still hear Nuna.

Faintly at first, but growing stronger, Elizapee then heard the deeper sound of men's voices. She heard Kiawak calling, then Poota's voice, and the shouts of two other hunters. Now, almost above her, she could hear Nuna talking to the men in breathless Inuktitut.

The only words she recognized were *Sharni, Uvilu,* and *Elizapee.*

Poota shouted down into a crack not far from her. "Elizapee! Are you there? Leah! Kowli! Do you hear me, Elizapeeee?"

Before she could answer him, she heard the huge ice shelf begin to groan and shift and sigh again. The violent lightning streaks went shooting in wild zigzag traces above her head. In front of her she heard another massive section of ice collapse. Elizapee screamed, then screamed again, in utter terror.

VI

BEFORE HER, ELIZAPEE COULD SEE SMALL BROKEN shards of ice come showering down like thousands of cubes spilling from refrigerator trays, each one flashing in the evening light as they fell around her.

Suddenly she saw a gash that had been torn open. Through it, she could see the sky. She wriggled toward the opening like a wet cat, then crawled out from the shallow cave where she had been trapped. Many hands reached down to help her. Rough ice scraped against her back, but in a moment she was free! Elizapee stood up straight, still trembling from head to foot. She felt like a circus clown, with more than a hundred big clams hanging around her middle and filling her parka hood and pockets, for she was still carrying every single clam she had found.

Poota yelled to her, "Did you see Sharni?"

"No," Elizapee cried. "I heard her call when the

first big noise came. Sharni!" she suddenly screamed in horror. "Where are you? Where's Uvilu?"

"Uvilu's over there. My father got her out. But where's Sharni?" Poota hurried along the edge of the broken ice fault.

"Be careful not to step too close," Tudlik cried as Poota leaned forward, calling Sharni's name.

Elizapee was being helped by Nuna to unbind her scarf and let the large weight of clams drop from the bottom of her parka. Then together they removed the others from her hood and pockets. Uvilu had already done the same.

Near a huge slump in the upper snow, Poota heard a human sound, and, jumping down, he started digging desperately. Everyone rushed to the place where Poota was digging and the men helped him, using their hands, using all the power they had.

They could no longer hear any living sounds and they were frightened when the tide put new pressure on the ice and they heard it sigh, then crack and sag again. This time it was a help to them, for one crack had widened enough for Poota to squeeze his body down beneath the ice.

"I think I can see her," he called to them in Inuktitut. "She looks hurt, and it's so dark down here. Don't walk on top near me. Go back, get back! I'm going to have to crawl on my belly to reach her."

Elizapee, above, could hear Poota gasping and the gravel and wet stones grinding beneath him.

"I can touch her now, but there is water coming in, water from the tide. It's rising all around us."

"Hurry," called his father through the crack.

"I'm trying to drag her," Poota called up to them.

"Sharni! Sharni! Help me!" they could hear him shout. "Do you understand me? Push with your feet if you can. We've got to get out of here right now!"

All those above heard a crablike scuttling on the frozen gravel just beyond them, then the sound of two bodies thrashing in the rising water!

"Help me, Sharni! Push with your feet! Hurry!" they heard Poota's voice calling. "Undo your clams. Forget the clams."

Then they could hear the gasping, scraping sound slowly drawing closer and closer to the crack.

Sharni's father, Tudlik, said to Kiawak, "Take a tight grip on my ankles, and kneel down behind me."

In this way Tudlik almost disappeared, hanging more than halfway down the dangerous ice crack.

Elizapee crouched in horror not far away. She was soaking wet and shuddering, gasping for breath, but too excited to feel the cold. She watched Tudlik's skin boots as they hung there upside down for ages while the shifting ice kept closing in.

Suddenly Tudlik grunted out some strange commands in Inuktitut, and Kiawak, with his strength, started drawing him cautiously upward out of the dripping icy jaws. With his big hands, Tudlik clasped Sharni's wrists. When Elizapee saw her, she let out a sob. Sharni's mitts were gone, her sleeves had been dragged back beyond her elbows, exposing her bruised arms. Her head, as it appeared above the ice, hung back as though she were already dead, her eyes half closed, her hair and clothing soaked.

When they had her lying stretched out on the snow, she looked pregnant, with her great load of clams still bound around her waist.

Kakak, Nuna's father, stepped down into the tumble of ice and helped Poota up. Poota's face now seemed as wrinkled and puckered as an old man's. His canvas hunting-parka cover was filthy with green seaweed stains and brown with dirt.

All the women from the camp were out and running toward them.

"Everyone, get away from this place right now!" Kiawak ordered, fearing another collapse, for the tide was rising and floating the ice.

Tudlik bent and picked up Sharni as though she weighed no more than a small child and carried her to the safety of the upper beach. Then Sharni's mother untied the woven belt from around her daughter's waist, and a great burden of clams fell to the snow.

Elizapee, who was with Uvilu beside Sharni, heard her moaning in her father's arms as he carried her into the warmth of their family tent.

"I hope she's going to be all right," Elizapee said.

"She comes from a strong family," Uvilu answered. "Almost never do her people get killed."

Once inside the protection of the big tent, Elizapee and Uvilu started changing their wet and grimy clothing while the men went back with two sacks to collect the clams. Maylee lit a pair of small Swedish Primus stoves, pumping them until their heads turned cherry red and gave off a roaring sound. On each, she placed a large pot full of ice.

After they washed their hands and faces and

brushed sand out of their hair, Uvilu and Elizapee pulled on dry pants. Two small children came in and told them that with help Sharni was sitting up, and her mother was changing her clothing for her. Sharni had said she was coming to the clam feast, no matter what.

Uvilu smiled at Elizapee. "I told you that girl came from a family full of courage."

Before long, everyone in the camp had gathered around Maylee and begun shucking the large clams, rinsing each one free of sand before placing it in one of the pots of simmering water.

"It was worth it," Uvilu told her grandfather. "I was really scared down under that ice, but look at the feast we gathered."

Her grandfather laughed and said, "You're just like your grandmother used to be. She'd do anything to help this family."

He smiled at Elizapee as she slipped a fat clam into the nearly boiling water. She smiled back and nodded to him, glad that they were all safely home with him again. A little later, Sharni's mother and father helped their daughter through the low tent door. There was a smile on each of their faces.

The rich, steamy smell that rose from the two large pots of clams was the best Elizapee could imagine. Old Paar pretended he could catch the smell between his hands and eat it. Everybody laughed. Laughter had become a rare sound in the camp since the three best snowmobiles had drifted away and the men's luck in hunting had run out.

Maylee passed her family some battered enamel dishes. Elizapee noticed that all the other families gathered for this feast had brought their own. Sharni was the first to receive her share of the steaming clams. She tried to smile at the others in spite of the raw, red gravel burns and bruises on her forehead and left cheek, and the swelling on her chin.

Uvilu received the second plate, and Elizapee received the third share. Then Poota was given his portion, for he had gone down beneath the ice to save Sharni.

The first half clam that Elizapee placed in her mouth tasted like the softest, richest food she had ever had. She sighed with pleasure, took the other half and swallowed it, and watched the glittering eyes and excited faces of the others who eagerly filled their mouths with real food for the first time after four long days and nights of hunger.

"All of this plenty for this feast was gathered by our young women at great risk to their lives," Kiawak announced to all the others in the tent. "We hunters will go out every day and hope the wind changes for us so we can equal their success."

Everyone slept well that night, their stomachs full of delicious clams. Early next morning, the hunters, feeling strong again, went out walking to the far end of the ice floe, which was breaking open, thanks to a new west wind. That afternoon, they took three large seals and, loading them on their sled, they smiled with relief and dragged them back to camp.

The bright spring sun circled them as it brushed

away the last of winter's darkness. The hard sea ice was softening, changing. Great sheets of the old ice were broken and carried away by the tide, and the whole sea west of Nesak Island turned sparkling blue.

At the camp, Elizapee was quickly settling in with her new family. She now knew everyone in the camp by name. Lao, their dog, often followed when she and Uvilu climbed the high rocks of the island. On clear days, they could see long, moving rafts of ice far out to sea. Eastward toward the mainland, the ice between it and their island was still solid, and snow lay like elegant white lace across the far blue mountains.

"Everyone in this camp is excited about crossing to the mainland," Poota told Elizapee. "The next big moon tide is coming, and we must go before it breaks the ice."

Poota was right. On the very edge of the melting snow, hardy fireweed and yellow Arctic poppies began to bloom, and many birds flocked in from the south, some of them landing on the island—snowbirds, old squaw ducks, geese, large tundra swans, curlew, even sandpipers. Elizapee watched a snowy owl nesting on the tundra.

"*Atai! Atai!* It's time to move," Kiawak called out to everyone. "Take down the winter tents. We are going to cross over to the fish lakes and rivers on the mainland. Tudlik and Kakak have fixed their old snowmobile, and we will tie our sleds behind it and walk beside them. We'll do the crossing as they did it in the old days."

When Poota translated his father's words to Elizapee,

he smiled with pleasure. She could tell that Poota was proud to be an Inuk, proud to be his father's son.

Early on the following morning, all the winter tents were down and their rough wood frames were tied and bundled carefully between protecting rocks to wait for another winter. The two sleds were piled high with the islanders' possessions, which were tightly lashed down. Then everyone started the journey on foot, the children running nearby over the hard-packed snow atop the ice toward the white boat that had been on the high beach since summer, and this they loaded with most of their food and camp equipment.

The conditions were perfect for their crossing. The snowmobile slowly dragged the sleds. The first was loaded with the few necessary things that the Nesak Island people treasured most. Their canoe was lashed onto the second sled and it also was packed full. The families numbered nineteen human beings of all ages, and their gentle husky, Lao. It was a bright, clear, windless day. They could see the mainland hanging like a distant blue-white dream before them.

When Elizapee found herself walking near Poota, he turned to her and said, "Not many people live like we do anymore." He sighed. "Most say we'll have to give up camp life soon and live in one of the settlements. Do you believe that's the way it should be?"

"I don't know," said Elizapee. "It is important about good health and food and schools. But it really should be the families who choose the kind of life they want to live, how they want to educate their children. I would freeze to death if I stayed outside in the Arctic

for even one winter night. Yet you and all these families have learned how to live this way over so many
generations. I'd call that being highly educated when
the subject is survival. Wouldn't you?"

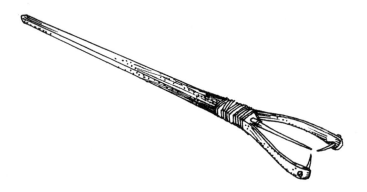

VII

ELIZAPEE HAD NEVER DREAMED THAT SHE COULD
walk so far or help to push the canoe and sleds so hard.
During her journey toward summer with the Nesak
Islanders, she no longer tried to measure distance in
miles or kilometers. Everyone was tired when they
reached the mainland, and they made camp late that
night.

The next morning, the old snowmobile with the
sleds was left with some of their goods in a cache
beside their old white hunting boat, which they had
left there last autumn high on the stony beach. They
started walking inland across snow patches and tundra,
skidding the loaded canoe toward the first dark patch
of open water that cut through the center of the river's
ice. From the bank, two of their hunters pulled the
canoe upstream with skin lines tied to its bow and
stern. Each man, sometimes helped by the boys and

stronger girls, took turns hauling the loaded canoe against the river's current.

Elizapee began to measure distance by sleeps. How many times had they put up their small summer tents and slept? Like Uvilu, she began to count these sleeps on her fingers instead of marking them in a diary.

Sometimes they walked in bright sunshine, sometimes in cloudy haze, sometimes in rainy weather that would turn to sleet, then snow, as the night cold came down around them. But it no longer bothered her, for she knew that summer was blowing north to them from somewhere south across these barren, treeless lands.

Elizapee often practiced Inuktitut as she walked, whispering over and over to herself new words she'd learned.

"Do I hear you talking to yourself again?" Uvilu laughed. "They say spirits sometimes talk to people who live out here in the lonely mountains and the inland plains. Perhaps they will answer you."

"I wish they would teach me how to speak Inuktitut to your parents and grandfather," Elizapee answered.

"You are speaking better now," Sharni told her. "This morning, my mother said she understood almost every word you said."

Elizapee smiled and hunched her heavy pack, with her sleeping bag rolled on top, a little higher so that the pack straps would not cut into her shoulders. She hoped that she would soon be as strong as Uvilu and Sharni.

In the mornings now, the hills were often hazy gray,

but usually cleared by noon. While they were on the move, the small children often fell asleep. Their fathers carried them across their shoulders, or their mothers cradled them in their hoods. Older girls held the hands of the younger children who toddled beside them. All the freshwater ponds were open now, and small flowers bloomed, making soft mauve and yellow patches in the sunlit tundra on the hillsides.

One day, they hurried ahead excitedly, eager to pass through a long valley, then cross a hill. From there, they could hear the sound of the upper river roaring lustily, the inland rapids the islanders had been longing to hear.

"Listen," Poota shouted to Elizapee. "Now you can hear the waterfalls. This is the best fish place, the place we've dreamed about all winter."

Did he call to me in Inuktitut or in English? Elizapee asked herself. I'm forgetting to notice the difference. That means I'm beginning to understand my own language.

"You'll like it up here on the inland," Uvilu told Elizapee. "You're going to meet some new young hunters and their families."

A large flock of geese rose into the air not far from them, but Poota and the other hunters scarcely looked at them, their thoughts were so much on the fish.

"See those stone circles across the river?" Uvilu asked. "They're old tent rings. We'll make camp there. I'll be glad to stop." She sighed. "I'm getting tired of walking, walking, every day, aren't you?"

"I seem to be getting better at it," Elizapee said. "I

feel stronger now than I ever have in all my life. When we first started upriver, my legs ached every day, but now I don't mind it. My pack doesn't seem half as heavy as it used to."

"You're changing a lot." Uvilu laughed happily. "Here, Lao!" she called to the gray bitch that wandered not far behind them, with two bulky packs of meat hanging one on either side of her back. Lao lay down near them to rest. "We should see the Tikirak people soon. Oh, I hope they will be there!"

"Who are they?" asked Elizapee.

Uvilu smiled and nudged Sharni, who was beside her.

"We mean the Tikirarmiut." Uvilu held up her first finger. "This is your *tikirak*. They have that name because they live on a long finger of land that points out to sea. You'll really like them. They are wonderful dancers."

"Any girl like you might find a husband among these young hunters," Sharni said to Elizapee. "You keep your eyes wide open for a good one."

Everyone seemed to walk faster, so eager were they to cross at the river's shallow ford.

When the sun was high, they climbed a hill that led down to the river's edge, where two of their men were pulling the canoe.

Elizapee gazed at the white, plunging falls flinging a haze of spray into the air before them. The river's waters frothed like silver, making small rainbows in the midday sun. Elizapee saw one big trout and then another as they leaped their way up the mighty river.

"It's going to be good," Poota called to her. "You bring us good luck, Elizapee. You can see the dear ones flashing silver as they crowd their way up the river. We'll rebuild the old stone caches and store many of these fish that we may catch here."

"Why does he call them 'dear'?" Elizapee asked Sharni.

"Because our hunters know that some animals have magical ears that can hear a long way off. Poota, all of us, need some of them for food to stay alive. He wants them to know we like them, we really need them. They'll understand we all need them, just as they need snow to eat or water."

Not far beyond them, Elizapee could see strangers—more than two dozen men, women, and children. The adults were busy putting up tents on a long, smooth gravel ridge. Down below them, in the river, Elizapee could see stones, each one the size of a shopping bag. They formed something that looked like the foundation of an old ruined house.

"There they are, the Tikirarmiut, our people."

Sharni smiled and nodded at Elizapee. "Now you'll see some fun! They've come here for the fishing just like us, and they've also hoped that we would join them. Often young hunters meet girls here. Then later they get married."

Uvilu, who was listening, held her hands against her bright red cheeks. "There's a boy over there with them. I can't see him yet, but . . . Oh, I hope he's there. I like him best of all!"

"Look," said Poota to Elizapee. "Some of their men

have taken off their boots and pants. They're wading into the river above their knees to close up the back of the fish trap with those big stones. No one knows how old that trap is, but it seems to have belonged to these Tikirak people and we Nesak Islanders forever. This has always been our summer meeting place." Glancing at his sister, he added, "Have you seen Ohaktok yet?"

"No, but I'll just die if he isn't here."

"Don't worry, I see Ohaktok over there," said Poota. "See him going into the river to help open the front entrance to the trap?" He laughed. "I'll bet that water's freezing cold."

Uvilu glanced at her brother slyly. "Elizapee can learn to dance the round dance with Ohaktok's brother. He's a good dancer."

"She can learn the round dance with me," said Poota. "She doesn't need him to teach her anything."

Everyone from the Nesak camp hurried toward their Tikirak friends. Each one shook every other person's hand, even the hands of the smallest newborn babies carried in their mothers' hoods. They had not seen each other since the last fish moon had faded and eleven other moons had come and gone.

Maylee and Uvilu, with help from young Emik and Elizapee, put up their tent, as did all the other families. Elizapee counted a dozen tents placed with their entrances toward the river. In a strange way, it felt to her like being in a big city again.

"I wonder if anyone of these people will recognize me," Elizapee said to Uvilu.

When Elizapee had done her part in helping to set up camp, she ran down to the fish weir with Uvilu, Sharni, and three girls from the other camp. The tide was flowing up the river, carrying in schools of bright, new, big, red-bellied Arctic trout. Elizapee could see many of them slipping like swift shadows beneath the water into the newly opened entrance of the weir trap.

The fishermen from both camps sat nodding, pointing, and whispering together as they watched the oncoming fish and sharpened the triple points on their strange-looking spears.

Finally, Kiawak and an older man from the Tikirak camp signaled each other and, taking off their boots and pants, they stepped into the icy water and quickly closed with stones the entrance to the fish weir. All the men, young and old, then climbed down inside the weir, wincing when they first felt the icy water. The girls and women hurried down after them and, smiling, formed a semicircle on each shore around the weir.

Elizapee watched Poota. She saw him raise his spear until its points were just above the water. He shaded his eyes against the sun and waited. Suddenly he plunged his spear downward, then lifted it—he had missed. He changed his position so that the sun was behind him.

Elizapee saw Kiawak stab downward and come up with a huge, silver fish struggling on the points of his spear. With the spear's shaft held beneath his arm, he used both hands to release the fish from the outer points. Then he grasped it in one hand. Taking three fast steps forward, he flung it straight at Maylee. She screamed, then laughed, as she caught it, wriggling and slippery in her hands.

"*Atai!*" Poota shouted, as he flung his first big red-bellied fish straight at Elizapee.

She caught it, but it wriggled and slipped from her grasp. Sharni lunged forward, trying to pick it up, but Elizapee was too fast for her and, kneeling, caught it by the gills. The women, watching both of them, let out a cheer.

"You're getting quick." Sharni laughed. "You're getting to be one of us. Everyone likes you. These Tikirak people, they'll like you, too."

When the men had taken nearly two hundred fish, they stopped. It was time to reopen the weir and let the rest of those sleek creatures go on their way upstream to spawn.

On the stony banks of the river, the women and girls sat or squatted together, cleaning the fish. First, they split them open so that they looked like giant red-and-silver butterflies. Then they tied them like clothing onto long sealskin lines between the tent tops so that they would dry and stiffen in the night wind. Later they would put these fish inside half-a-dozen ancient stone caches, each as big around as a large tractor tire and higher than a hunter's waist. These stone storage huts had probably been built when the earliest fishing families had come here perhaps a thousand years ago.

Already Elizapee, who was busy with the others learning to clean fish fast, could smell the rich aroma of fresh fish stew drifting out of almost every tent.

"Why are the men taking our tent down?" Elizapee suddenly asked Uvilu in alarm.

The girls near her laughed. Uvilu answered. "They are going to arrange three tents together and make a dance house so we can feast, then dance, then feast again inside. My grandfather, Paar, is warming up the drum to make its skin tight, and one of the Tikirak women has her accordion with her. She is very good at playing. Oh, we'll all have a wonderful time, you'll see. I hope this dance time never ends!"

And that's just the way it seemed to Elizapee. She thought it was the best and most exciting night she had ever had in all her life. The feast of stew and fresh raw fish, the laughing, the dancing, the running between the tents, the singing, made her feel that she had become a true Inuk. At last, she had found her own people.

Each person danced freestyle, starting by just tapping his or her soft skin boots in beautiful ways that Elizapee at first found very difficult to do. She watched as Poota and another young hunter faced each other, studying the cleverness of his dance steps.

The watchers gasped and sighed in wonder at the skill that these male dancers showed. The girls and women did not compete with each other in their dancing, but swayed and tapped their feet to the rising rhythm of the drum.

Uvilu's young hunter, Ohaktok, from the Tikirak camp, seemed never to take his eyes off her. Uvilu blushed and smiled shyly at her friends, but did not seem to look at Ohaktok even once.

"She knows what she's doing," Sharni whispered in

Elizapee's ear. "Those young Tikirak men say they prefer marrying quiet girls, but look how their own girls laugh and dance and sing."

When the sky was brightening and the sun was about to rise above the hills beyond the river, Poota's grandfather, Paar, who had fallen asleep, woke up. He drank a cup of tea while people called, "*Unikakuka-laurli!*" meaning they wanted him to tell a story.

The big three-together tent became quiet.

"Once, a long time ago," Paar began, "there was a man living at our Nesak camp. He went hunting on the ice alone. Before long, he saw the marks of a bear's paws. He followed them. Then suddenly he saw another set of bear tracks. And still other sets joined the first two until there were six sets of large tracks all together. He had never seen so many bear prints at one time. He followed them, even though it was getting dark and he was feeling more and more afraid.

"Then, in front of him, he saw a soft glow. It was lamplight shining through an igloo wall. But this igloo was not shaped like a rounded Inuit house. This igloo was very tall and pointed at the top, with two, long wind-tunnel entrances, one to go inside and the other to come out. All six bear tracks led to the going-inside tunnel.

"The hunter waited until it was truly dark, then climbed very cautiously on top of the going-inside tunnel, where he gently poked a small peephole in the snow-house wall. Putting his eye to the opening, he could see the last of the bears taking off its heavy, hairy white parka and white leggings. There they all sat laughing and talking in a row, looking just like naked human beings on their sleeping bench. Beside them sat two female bears. One of the mother bears was feeding her baby.

"These great bears," Paar said, "spoke perfect Inuktitut. They were showing their teeth and sneezing, belching and grunting like ordinary humans. One of them was making faces, and another was tapping a strange rhythm on the drum." Poota's grandfather beat a strange rhythm on his drum.

"The female bear with the baby turned, and the hunter from Nesak Island could see that she was not nursing a bear cub, but a real human child, with plump red cheeks and a striped caribou bonnet with horn tassels sewn on it. The human child looked up and called out a warning to the bears, pointing to the hunter's blinking eye at the small hole in their snowhouse wall.

"Two of the biggest bears jumped up, and with a roar pulled on their huge white leggings and furry parkas, and rushed out of the going-in tunnel to try and catch the human. But by this time, the hunter had leaped down and was running faster than any of the bears.

"When the weary hunter returned to our island, he had this advice for all of us: 'The more closely you watch the animals, the more surely you will discover that they are almost like ourselves. They like to talk and dance and sing. If you don't believe that, just listen to the snowbirds and young wolves. They all like to chase and play as we do. Yes, you must carefully study their ways.'

"You all saw those geese and caribou as we walked

past them yesterday. They did not run from us or fly, because they knew that at that time we were not hunting. But if any one of you had tried to slip a gun out of its case, they would have quickly fled away. The animals know so much about us that they need to ask no questions. They are each of them filled with some ancient kind of understanding. After all, they have to be intelligent. They are hunters, we are hunters. And we all must share this world together."

"I wouldn't mind sharing my world with that Ohaktok," Uvilu whispered to Elizapee as the two girls crawled inside their sleeping bags and fell asleep at once.

VIII

AFTER THE FISHING, UVILU, SHARNI, AND ELIZAPEE
were delighted to find that the two camps were staying
together to share in the inland hunting. There would
be more dancing, they hoped. The long days of summer were fading now.

For more than a week, they continued along the
course of the river, facing eastward toward the rising
sun. The nights were cold and starting to turn dark
gray, and in the morning, there were thin white rims
of ice on the edges of the smaller ponds.

Elizapee looked up at some flocks of geese on the
far hills and wondered whether, if she had the power
to fly, she would choose to rise up and travel with
them to spend the winter in the warmth of Louisiana,
Alabama, or Texas, where she knew they went. No,
she answered, smiling to herself. I'm grateful to be
here with my own people, just where I belong. I'm

learning how to live a whole new life where almost everything interests and excites me.

Elizapee thought of her years of growing up in the south, of the kindly couple who had acted almost as her parents. They had taken her with their own two children to a summer cottage by a lake where they had all enjoyed a life of swimming and picnics in the woods, and nights in front of a warm crackling camp fire eating buttered ears of corn. She thought of her hospital visits for tests that finally proved her free of tuberculosis, of returning to the school where she had spent the winters, except for school vacations with her southern family. Sometimes Elizapee felt half like a member of that southern family and half like someone from this Inuit-Eskimo camp. It seemed to her in some ways that she belonged to all of them and they all belonged to her.

"There are so many feathers on the ground now," Elizapee said to Sharni.

"That's because midsummer is molting time, when all the adult geese must lose their feathers, especially their strongest wing and tail feathers." Sharni stooped to pick up one and handed it to Elizapee. "Now that these have fallen out, the geese can't fly."

"Why are we turning north now instead of east toward the morning sun?"

"You ask Poota," Sharni said. "His father and mine decided to go this way."

"Why?" Elizapee asked Poota.

"Because they hope to find the flocks of black-necked geese with white cheek patches and the snow geese that in this season have molted and cannot fly. And also we are going toward the goose pens," Poota replied.

"What are they?" Elizapee whispered to Sharni.

"They are old stone walls about as high as your waist, built very long ago," Sharni explained. "If we find the geese, we will make a big half-circle behind them and try to herd them through the entrance to the pens. It's not easy, but when the geese are all inside, we will rush forward and build up the stone entrance and there will be hundreds and hundreds of geese inside. Only a few will be able to jump or half fly over the wall."

"Everything is so different for nomad families," said Elizapee. "You can't go to a supermarket out here. That's a huge store where you can buy a chicken that has been killed by someone else then machine-wrapped in plastic."

"No," said Uvilu. "That sounds very strange. Inuit living off the land have to use all the intelligence they have to think of ways to feed their families."

"Listen, you can hear them," Poota called, and as they topped the next hill, Elizapee looked down and saw hundreds and hundreds of blue geese, which were close relatives to the white snow geese and flocked with them.

"Separate," Tudlik signaled to all of them, as he and Kiawak hurried out to either end of a big half-circle. Every man, woman, and child old enough to walk spread out about thirty steps apart.

Some called to each other, some laughed and

coughed, and babies cried. It didn't seem to matter. The geese watched the newcomers for some moments, then, crowding close together, the birds began to waddle, slowly at first, then faster, honking to each other. There were some young birds with them.

"I hope your father and mine remember where this goose pen is," Uvilu said to Sharni. "I can't see it anywhere."

"They probably know," called Poota, "but I can't see it either."

"*Takuviuk?* You see it?" Kiawak pointed north.

For the first time, Elizapee and the others could see the large stone pen. "Once I saw a girl on a farm I visited down south and she was driving three geese toward a gate just like we are."

"What's a farm?" called Nuna. "I've heard of farms."

"I'll tell you later," Elizapee answered her, for now they could scarcely hear each other because of the excited honking of the geese.

The humans started to move closer together, arms outspread toward the flock. First one lead gander, then several of the larger geese, began to follow one another into the narrow entrance of the stone pen. They were quickly trailed by all the rest.

Poota, Kiawak, Tudlik, and the other hunters, with the women and children, crouched down and rushed to the entrance of the pen. They blocked it closed with stones.

The men climbed over the ancient, mossy walls and began to twist the necks and then fling out their selection of the plumpest of the geese. These molting birds fell on the gray-green tundra beyond the pen almost without a flutter, and the girls, like their mothers, gathered up the geese, holding them by the necks until they themselves looked like huge white down pillows.

"That's enough!" called Kiawak.

"Don't take any more than we need," Ohaktok called out, then flung the last goose at Uvilu, who laughed and caught it in the air.

Tudlik and Poota opened the stone entrance. Soon the geese went flocking out, not entirely to safety, for they and their young would still have to face dangers from wolves, foxes, owls, and falcons.

"Their feathers are growing now," Poota told Elizapee. "Soon they'll all go south before the snow flies. But I hope they'll return again next spring."

"Oh, what a feast we will have tonight," said Elizapee.

"And for many nights to follow," Poota added.

Ten days later, their packs felt lighter, for all the goose meat was gone.

As they were walking farther upriver, Poota came to Elizapee and pointed. "Can you see something over there?"

"See what?" Elizapee asked.

"*Tuktuit,*" he answered. He was testing her.

"I can't see any caribou. Can you?"

"Yes. I see maybe *avatit.*" He twice opened the fingers of both his hands. "Now I see *avatitlu sita-*

mutlu, twenty-four of them, in front of you."

"Oh, I see them now," Sharni whispered, for she had crept up behind them. "See their white belly hair? They will make beautiful stripes on our new winter parkas."

"Maybe I see one over there." Elizapee squinted her eyes and pointed.

"No, that's a rock," said Poota. "The *tuktuit* are feeding to the left of that long stone."

"Oh, I see them now—their white bellies. Many of them seem to be looking at us. This whole land is so flat," Elizapee whispered, "how can you ever hope to get close to them?"

"It won't be easy," Poota agreed. "They know we are here and they are already nervous of our thoughts. They know inside themselves that we are planning to hunt them. See those stones piled one on top of the other? They are called *inukshuks*, 'likenesses of humans.' Those rocks were piled up long ago to look like hunters. The women and girls and children will move between them. Go with Uvilu and Sharni," he told Elizapee. "They will show you what to do. I am going with the hunters. We will stay in the river valley out of sight of the caribou and you will drive them slowly to us. You will take the dog," said Poota. "Keep a harness on her so she won't run and frighten those dear *tuktuit*. Tie her mouth if she starts whining."

Uvilu showed Elizapee where to hide halfway between two of the stone *inukshuks*. Lying flat on the soft, dry tundra, Elizapee watched the movements of the caribou. They seemed aware of the women. They were nervous and alert.

"When they come close to you, first kneel, then stand up very gently," Uvilu told Elizapee. "They will stop and watch you, ears cocked forward. Then wave your arms a little to encourage them to move along the way we want them to—between our two old lines of stones. When they see the next stone *inukshuks*, they will think that they are humans, too. Then they will keep moving farther down our narrowing path to where the men will be waiting for them, hiding at the river crossing. You follow slowly after them to keep them moving. Don't hurry, though, Elizapee. Don't panic those dear creatures. We and they have all day long to reach the river."

The sun was setting when Elizapee finally arrived on top of the high gravel bank and looked down to the water. The silent hunt was over. Not one shot had been fired. Noise would have frightened the caribou. These nomad hunters had carefully taken only the *tuktuit* that they needed. When a caribou passed between two large rocks, one of the men had reached out and killed it silently with his iron-tipped spear.

"We have as many as we need," Kiawak said to Maylee and Elizapee and the other women, as they came in toward the hunters.

"I have a small gift for you," Poota whispered to Elizapee when they were alone. "It is the fourth moon since you came to us. It is not a very good gift, but it is the best that I could make for you. It has a lucky caribou-horn handle and its blade is shaped like the half face of the moon. Be careful," Poota warned. "The knife's edge is sharp. I shaped it from an old saw blade Kakak gave me. I give it to you now because it is the time when you will need it. It is an *ulu*, a woman's knife."

"Did you really make it for me?" Elizapee looked at him closely.

"Yes. But don't let everyone know that at first, or they will make jokes about me, about us."

Elizapee smiled as she cautiously slipped the sharp knife up her wide parka sleeve and walked away toward Maylee, Sharni, and Nuna, who were already squatting by the fallen caribou.

"I have a spare *ulu* from my aunt," said Nuna. "I will lend it to you, and Maylee will show you how to skin a *tuktu*. She is best at it."

"I have an *ulu* of my own," said Elizapee, shyly slipping the new gift out of her sleeve.

"Oh!" said Maylee. "That looks like a good one, made by someone young, maybe, but someone clever."

"Yes," said Elizapee. "He warned me to be careful. It is sharp."

Maylee smiled, then took the new *ulu* from her and dulled its sharp edge against a stone. "Remember, sharp for cutting fish and birds and cloth, but dull for skinning hides and fur. You don't want to cut any slits or make holes in them."

Maylee began to show Elizapee the ancient

women's art of skinning. She worked fast, but with great care and skill.

Sharni and Uvilu, who were now busy skinning, too, looked slyly at Elizapee. Sharni said, "We can guess who gave you that new *ulu*."

Elizapee put up her hood for protection against the mosquitoes, then rolled up her parka sleeves and began to work like the others. Awkwardly at first, she cut, then separated the warm, bluish inner hide from the animal's flesh, amazed that they came apart so easily.

She brushed away the mosquitoes from her wrists, then said, "Oh, I made a slit in the skin!" Elizapee felt ashamed.

"Don't worry too much," said Uvilu, examining the small cut. "We can sew that up with sinew. But be careful." She took Elizapee's new *ulu* and dulled its edge a bit more on a stone. "It has a nice handle. I think my brother made this for you. Giving it to you means he likes you a lot. Maybe it means he wants you to help him with the caribou he takes when he is grown up. You know what I mean?"

"Maybe," said Elizapee, trying not to look too pleased, as she went on skinning the *tuktu*, being very careful not to make another slit.

With the Tikirarmiut, the Nesak Islanders held one last great feast of caribou, and there was drumming, accordion playing, dancing, singing, storytelling. Elizapee had come to know and like many of the Tikirarmiut. But now the elders said it was the time to part.

Next morning, their tents were taken down, and some people, young and old, wept as the two camps moved apart, for they would not see each other for eleven moons.

The Nesak people, Elizapee's people, had decided to leave the inland and return to the coast. They loaded their canoe with caribou meat, an abundance of tightly rolled caribou hides for winter clothing, and their tents. With young Emik in the bow and old Paar steering in the stern, the canoe started slowly down the river ahead of the Nesak Islanders toward the sea and the island that they hoped would be their winter home again. Every evening those walking along the riverbank would meet the canoe at a new campsite.

The journey down on the long river's course sometimes forced them to scramble over great scatterings of rocks. It took them eleven long days. They often had to carry the youngest children on their backs. They ate little during the day, but each night, Elizapee, like the others, delighted in the rich marrow sucked from the caribou bones and the simmering caribou stews. Most mornings when they rose, the autumn moon stayed strong in the dark blue sky and the riverbanks and hills beyond were white from newly fallen snow.

It was turning cold when they reached the lonely seashore and headed for their white boat and their cache of winter oil-stove fuel. Just beneath the tide line lay some of the best green stone for carving. They could see Nesak standing gray on the horizon. A heavy wind swept in at all of them. Elizapee shaded her eyes. New black ice had formed, covering the water almost as far as she could see.

The dark time was coming now, and soon they would cross the dangerous-looking ice to the hat-shaped island of Nesak and live there until spring. Elizapee wondered if she could stand a winter there without the sun. There were only a few schoolbooks to read, there was no television, no basketball, and always the search for the very food that they needed to stay alive. Perhaps, she thought, she should have done as George had suggested when he had brought her here—visited for a little while, then gone back to the city and lived in the school. But then she remembered how lonely that life had been.

The Nesak people worked together quickly, putting up and weighing down their summer tents, using stones from old camp rings. Small Primus stoves now heated all four dwellings. After eating, Elizapee left her socks and sweater on and wrapped herself tightly in her sleeping bag. Just before she drifted off to sleep, she decided to put on her hat as well for warmth.

Early next morning, she woke to the sound of Poota coming back inside the tent with his father. He was shuddering and had his hands jammed deep inside his pockets. The thin tent walls were flapping noisily as the sea wind hammered at them.

"Oh, it's cold out there," said Poota, "and we couldn't even see open water until we climbed the hill." Poota looked worried. "It's too bad this thin black ice has formed. Now we are going to have to wait until it gets strong enough to let us skid the boats out over it, hoping to reach open water and then travel on to Nesak."

"I don't really understand all of that," Elizapee answered him. "But it sounds frightening to me."

Emik and the other young ones ran zigzag through the melting whiteness and delighted in the early winter trails they left behind, while their fathers and their brothers and some of the women broke off chunks of the green stone. They would have to wait for a dozen days or so until the ice grew strong enough to cross over at least partway to the island. During this quiet time, with the simplest tools—a hatchet, a hacksaw, and some rough and smooth files—they cut and shaped wonderful carvings, ideas they had been storing up in their minds. Cutting the stones kept them warm and seeing their thoughts take shape made the days pass quickly.

Kiawak made a beautiful large carving of a mother and child, and when it was finished, Maylee seal-oiled it and sanded it, polishing it until the stone looked like rich green jade. Poota made a running bear that seemed so alive it might leap into the water. Sharni made an owl with wings outstretched and, carved from a piece of antler, three white eggs beneath it.

Everyone made carvings, splendid carvings; even Elizapee, with some help from Poota, made a small stone man walking.

"He looks stiff," she said to Poota.

"He's supposed to look stiff," Poota answered. "He's nervous, he's walking on thin ice!"

Everyone laughed at that. These Inuit from Nesak were no ordinary carvers. They were recognized as being among the very best of all. They could hardly wait to take their pieces to Iqaluit and see how much trade these carvings would bring.

IX

FOR ALMOST ONE WHOLE MOON, THE MEN AND women worked repairing the canvas canoe. Each woman cut and sewed new caribou winter clothing for everyone in her family.

Finally, when the ice seemed strong enough, they decided to break camp. The men went down to load the canoe and boat. The women stayed back, quickly taking down the tents and packing their few possessions. They carried everything onto the beach and helped load it tight inside the boat and canoe. The grandfather and Emik each lugged an armload of the hunters' seal harpoons, ice chisels, rifles, and snow knives. They packed them into the bow of the canoe.

The men had placed three short, round, wooden rollers under their old boat, named *Oopik*, for she was stubby and white, shaped like a snowy owl. They pulled at the props that had held her safely upright above the tide. Clinging to her sides, they made the white boat roll smoothly out onto the thick shore ice. Emik was the one to catch each roller as it came out from beneath the end of the boat. He then ran forward and slipped it underneath the bow again, then ran back and caught the middle roller as it came spinning out the end.

Elizapee said to Uvilu, who was pushing the boat beside her, "That young brother of yours is a fast runner and good at catching the rollers."

"Yes," gasped Uvilu, who was pushing hard. "I don't know how he does it without falling on this ice."

"*Taima!* Stop!" Poota's father called to all of them, and they stopped pushing *Oopik*.

Four of the hunters walked quickly back to the canoe, for now the hours of daylight were growing short, and they all wanted to reach Nesak Island before darkness could overtake them.

"Seven of us will fit into the big canoe," said Kiawak. "Come, Tudlik, Maylee, Poota, Uvilu, Sharni, and Elizapee. All of us pushing this canoe together will move it quickly until the ice becomes too weak to hold us. The heavier boat with everyone else can follow us and use our path until they, too, break through."

The canoe slid easily forward on its long wooden underkeel.

"It sounds scary to me," Elizapee whispered to Uvilu. "But I'm glad your father chose me to come with you." Lao was running beside her.

"It's because he knows you're a strong runner,"

Uvilu answered. "Sharni and her father, they're strong, too."

No words were spoken as they started forward pushing the canoe. The others stood beside *Oopik*, waiting.

Later, when Elizapee looked back, the white boat and the group of people around it seemed very small, and yet she could tell that they were now following in the canoe's icy path. Both canoe and boat were moving out toward the open water.

Head down and pushing, Elizapee noticed that the new ice beneath her feet was clear and black as a polished floor and looked like a thin pane of glass between herself and the deep black sea below.

"Hold tight to the side of the canoe," Poota called to Elizapee. "We are going to run. We could break through any time now. If you hear the ice cracking beneath us, help run the canoe forward even faster. Then be ready to jump inside the canoe and squat down and hold onto both sides to steady it!"

Elizapee increased her pace. Poota's idea sounded more dangerous to her than anything she had ever tried before.

"I never dreamed," she gasped to Uvilu, "that I'd be doing something like this."

Sharni, on the other side of the canoe, laughed. "I like running on ice before it breaks. Let's go, let's go!"

Elizapee looked up, and not far in front of them, she could see the long, flat edge of the ice. It was bumpy and frosted white. Beyond it there was open water rippling as though a million silver fish were flipping nervously in the cold west wind.

Suddenly she could feel the ice begin to sag and sink beneath her feet.

"Run!" yelled Kiawak.

"Run, run," shouted Poota, "fast as you can!"

They ran together, skidding the long canoe between them as the thin salt ice bellied down beneath their scrambling feet. They were three on each side of the canoe with Kiawak pushing at the stern, ready to warn them as the danger increased.

"Keep moving! Run! It's thinner here," he called.

There was a sound of cracking, and fine white lines went shooting out across the dead black ice.

"Run. Push!" yelled Tudlik. "Try to reach the edge."

With each running step, they knew that they were moving onto thinner ice. Suddenly the ice broke and water began to flood around them. The canoe sagged down.

"Jump in! Jump in!" Kiawak bellowed, and Lao leaped in as though she had been the first to understand his words.

Elizapee already had a tight grip on the side, and using that she scrambled quick as a cat inside the canoe. Then, crouching, she held each of the canoe's frail sides to steady it. All the others were busy doing the same, and now the old, overloaded canoe sat like a heavy duck, surrounded by shattered ice.

"How are we . . . ever . . . going to get out . . . of here?" Elizapee asked Poota, who, like herself, was gasping from their long, desperate run.

"We've got to force our way forward until we reach

that floe edge up ahead, where we can get this canoe into open water."

Poota looked at his father, who was now kneeling in the square stern of the canoe, examining their outboard engine. "How hard is it to break that ice in front with the chisel?" Kiawak asked his son.

Poota rose carefully in the bow, and started chopping downward with the long chisel, breaking through the ice. "I can make an opening. The ice is thinner here."

"Keep breaking it," his father said, "and I'll try to start this motor."

Kiawak, like many Inuit, was clever with old motors. They heard him pulling at the starting rope a dozen times before it wheezed, then coughed, then growled coldly back to life. Kiawak turned the engine this way and that so that the propeller would chew up the thin ice near it.

Slowly the long canoe began to ease forward, following the line that Poota was cutting with the chisel.

"Rock the boat, everyone," Kiawak called. "Rock carefully, but hard!"

Tudlik and Sharni helped, pushing with their paddles. The weight of the rocking canoe helped to break the ice around its sides, and they crept toward the frosted floe edge that spread its icy white fingers out to touch the cold black waters. The canoe's motor continued to make a low, gargling sound as it forced the heavily loaded canoe forward.

When Elizapee looked back through the gloom, she could see that the white boat, *Oopik*, was still following them and had not yet crashed through the ice. The people who stood beside *Oopik* looked very small and faraway.

Suddenly, Elizapee felt the canoe's bow swing sideways as Poota's chisel finally freed them from the ice.

Kiawak cut off the engine and let the canoe drift with the wind.

"*Oopik* is still a long way off," said Tudlik.

Elizapee saw Sharni look up at the half ball of dark-orange sun now disappearing into a thick, gray blanket of Arctic fog.

"It's getting late," said Kiawak.

"My wife and son are with that other boat," said Tudlik. "I'd like to wait for them, but we can't. Heavier ice is drifting toward us on this tide. No, we cannot wait."

"They will be safe on top of the heavier ice," Kiawak agreed. "They may have to turn back. But we must try to reach the island before dark. We can't go back now."

Elizapee shuddered from the cold, wishing she had on her new winter clothing, which was in the boat. She heard the outboard engine roar into life again. The tattered, ice-chewed canvas bow of the canoe swung south, and they moved cautiously through broken paths of drifting ice. The sun slid down behind the western hills, and they could just barely see the dark outline of their island looming in the night fog.

"There is no open water near the island." Poota pointed.

Kiawak spoke in rapid Inuktitut to all the rest.

"Elizapee, my father says we can't stay here or go

to the island. We'll get caught in sharp moving ice that's coming at us from the west. It will cut this canoe to pieces if we stay."

No more words were said as they turned and headed east. Now, at least, the icy wind was at their backs. Elizapee looked out from her fur hood and saw their boat *Oopik* still perched up on the ice, so far away it looked like a painted wooden toy. She saw no humans near it. Probably they were inside the boat, trying to find shelter from the rising wind.

It was almost totally dark when they reached the eastern end of the ice. Kiawak shut off the engine and let the canoe drift until its bow touched the floe edge. Poota tested the ice with the long chisel, then, seeing it was strong enough, he stepped out cautiously and held the bow.

"We're going to have to wait here," Kiawak said, "unless the tide drives that drift ice against us so hard that we have to try and move again."

Tudlik agreed.

"*Kaapunga,* I'm hungry," said Kiawak. All of them had worked hard all day and were suffering from exhaustion and lack of food.

Maylee shivered, then said, "Almost all our food was put into the other boat. We never thought we would be separated. I have only this," she said, and drew two pie-shaped bannocks from her heavy woolen trade shawl. "There's a leg of caribou meat up in the bow."

"We've been short of food before," said Tudlik.

Elizapee whispered to Uvilu, "I've only been short of food once in my life, during those four days before we found the clams. I hope I'll never be that hungry again."

"See that white line moving toward us on the water?" said Kiawak, pointing. "It's ice floating fast toward us. Get the canoe out of the water. Haul it up onto the floe edge."

When she had helped them and the canoe was safe, Elizapee bit her lip in fear.

"Don't get excited," Sharni warned her. "It may not be too bad, although that wind is getting stronger."

When the fast-drifting tidal ice struck the floe edge where they stood, the floe trembled beneath them and there was a sound like a giant grinding his jaws. One piece of ice as big as the top of a grand piano slid up on top of the floe near them. Elizapee and the others leaped back from it in terror as another, then another floor-sized piece of ice pushed up, then fell, stacking one on top of the other like a giant's deck of playing cards. When the great weight of these became too heavy, the whole stacked pile crashed down, sending shards of ice and water over their feet.

"Run to the canoe!" yelled Kiawak. "Everyone get a tight grip on the canoe. Turn it, pull it. Move, move! We've got to try to get away from here! *Tuavi, tuavi!* Hurry, hurry!"

Now Lao ran close beside them as though she, too, were desperate to help them pull.

X

DRIVEN BY FEAR AND THE THIN ICE BENEATH THEM, all seven raced again through the early winter darkness, skidding the canoe on its long keel across the ice. Sometimes slipping, sometimes sliding, eastward on this newly frozen water, they were headed for some place that none of them could see and that Elizapee could only hope would save them.

"Stop! Listen!" Kiawak called out.

The canoe glided to a stop. It was water they could hear, somewhere out in front of them, lapping like cold tongues against the broken edge of ice.

"Be careful! Hold tight to the canoe!" Kiawak warned. "The ice could break."

Elizapee shuddered. Why was she here in this impossibly dangerous place when she could be safe in a warm bed somewhere far to the south?

"The ice is sagging, jump into the canoe," yelled Tudlik. "It's breaking! Jump in! Jump in!"

Elizapee slipped as she tried to scramble into the canoe. This is the worst moment in my whole life, she thought, as she saw three long cracks go zigzagging across the ice away from them, then a dozen more. The canoe tipped, then sank into the water. Elizapee just managed to leap in.

"Get the paddles," Tudlik called. "Everyone stay kneeling. That broken ice is cutting in toward us."

They managed to paddle only a few strokes before they heard Kiawak thrashing at the engine cord. Finally the outboard let out a roar. He guided the canoe down the widening path of open water that now stretched before them. Kiawak steered it as far as they could go, then he stopped the engine and lifted its propeller clear of the broken ice.

"Now we're at the mercy of this wind," he called. "If you have any prayers to say, you say them now!"

Elizapee could hear the thin, sharp ice shattering, then cutting and grinding, like heavy broken plate glass, along the canvas sides of their canoe.

When that terrible sound faded behind them, they were free of the ice, but they drifted in the darkness. Above their heads, the wind was tearing huge holes in the clouds, exposing wide patterns of shining stars, but not the moon.

Poota pointed out the North Star to Elizapee. It was directly behind them.

So, she thought, it's good. Aloud, she said, "We're floating south. This wind is driving us south."

"You're right about that," Poota answered. "But south is exactly where we do not want to go."

"Why?" asked Elizapee. "It should be warmer in the south, no ice. Some winters on the Great Lakes we get very little ice, they say."

"To our south lies Hudson Bay," said Poota. "Have you seen it on a map? It's huge. If we get caught in those powerful tides, we will be swept away forever. A canoe like this could never stand the winds and ice down there."

"Is there nothing we can do?" Elizapee asked, rising cautiously onto her knees and gripping the thwart, for she found the thin canoe made her backside freezing cold.

"We can only hope that the wind will change and blow us toward the land," said Sharni, "or at least calm down by morning."

"What about the others from our camp that we left behind?"

"I believe they were able to turn the white boat around on top of the ice," Poota told her, "and skid it back to the shore again."

"I pray they're safe," said Elizapee. "Why doesn't your father start the motor again?"

"He won't do that in all this darkness," Uvilu told her. "We might run into drifting ice and break the propeller."

Elizapee was so exhausted from all the running and the pushing that she must have slept, huddled against Uvilu, feeling her welcome warmth against her side.

When she and Uvilu awoke, their thighs and buttocks seemed to be frozen or still asleep. Maylee had to take their hands and pull them into another position.

Elizapee eased back until she once more rested against the thwart.

"Get ready," Kiawak called to them. "We're going to run into ice again."

This time, Kiawak and Poota each took up a paddle, and Tudlik held the heavy chisel.

"You get ready," Sharni warned Elizapee. "We may get wet this time."

Elizapee watched the sharp white line of ice as it closed in on them through the first faint light of dawn. The wind was growing colder and stronger now. She heard that dreadful sound again, that fearsome grinding of sharp ice along the canoe at the waterline. Poota and Tudlik and Sharni worked with all their might to stave it off.

Kiawak stood up and called to them. "There is a small lake inside the ice not very far ahead of us. If we could work our way up this narrow crack, we might get inside that protective circle of ice and be safe until this wind dies down."

Tudlik used all his strength on the ice chisel, trying to open up a path. Sometimes he climbed out of the canoe onto one of the heavier pieces of ice and forced the bow back into the right channel.

As Poota tried desperately to help with his paddle, it suddenly split, then shattered, ruining the blade.

"Oh, that's bad!" cried Poota. "Very bad. We needed that paddle so much now."

"*Ayurnamat*, it can't be helped," others in the canoe called out, trying to make him know they did not think the ruining of the paddle was his fault. Sharni was still doing her best with the only other paddle, which she had taken from tired Kiawak.

At that moment, Elizapee heard the motor cord jerk hard once, twice, and on the third try, she heard the engine give a gurgling roar. Poota's father set the engine at its slowest speed.

"We have to use the engine now," Uvilu whispered, "because one of our paddles is gone."

As they worked their way toward the little lake, Elizapee felt a heavy bump that shook the canoe.

"My paddle's caught in the ice," cried Sharni. "The crack is closing."

Kiawak, to save the engine, cut off the power and lifted the propeller clear of the grinding ice. They all heard Sharni's paddle break. The crack was closing faster now, and it began to crush them.

First beside her right knee, then her left, Elizapee watched the canoe squeeze out of shape as its curved wooden ribs started to crack, then splinter. She could hear its canvas cover ripping as the icy water poured in on all of them.

"We're sinking, sinking! Get out!" yelled Kiawak, as he unscrewed the outboard motor and let it fall off the stern. "Get onto the ice! Save anything you can!"

Kiawak reached out and grasped Maylee's hand and pulled her onto the ice. Poota jumped free, and bending in one quick movement, he grabbed Elizapee's mitted hand and hauled her out of the sinking canoe. Her father caught Uvilu beneath the arms and dragged her to safety.

Tudlik had flung the long chisel away onto the ice.

Now he grabbed his daughter, Sharni, and two sleeping bags and the rope tied to the front of the crushed canoe as they fell together onto the ice.

"*Atai!* Grab this rope! Help me!" Tudlik shouted.

Elizapee and Sharni lunged at the rope and tried to pull like a whole team in a tug-of-war, but their feet kept slipping. Poota and Uvilu rushed to help them as Kiawak snatched up their rifles, harpoons, another half-sodden sleeping bag, and the roll of caribou sleeping skins, tumbling them across the ice before he jumped clear of the ruined canoe. Maylee laid her precious stone lamp and metal cooking pot on the ice, then she, too, grasped hold of the straining rope.

Tudlik, the strongest of them all, caught hold of the bow of the canoe with both his bare hands. Working desperately together, they drew the wreckage of the canoe onto the ice. Each one of them, except Elizapee, knew that these long, broken, twisted scraps of wood and canvas might be their only chance to stay alive.

XI

AS THE COLD YELLOW LIGHT OF DAWN GREW stronger, they squatted shoulder to shoulder, facing each other in a circle, trying to gather strength from the idea that they were still together and alive.

Finally, Kiawak stood up and looked around. "Be careful where you walk," he said. "This moving ice is thin and may be growing thinner as we drift south."

The women rose stiffly and busied themselves, gathering and sorting out to dry the few things they had managed to save.

"These three caribou sleeping skins are wet, but not soaking," said Maylee as she and Sharni hauled them out of their damp canvas-covered bags.

"Uvilu and Elizapee, you two help Poota pull the broken canoe frame apart," said Kiawak. "We'll use the keel and the four top framing boards to form a kind of three-sided prop and we'll tie up the sleeping bags.

This wind is wild and strong. They shouldn't take too long to dry."

"We're lucky we could grab them. I don't think we'd stay alive out here without them." Maylee looked at the three girls and said, "It's going to be hard for seven of us to survive on this moving ice, even with those three sleeping bags, and we have little food."

"At least we've got a chance," said Sharni. "We'll do everything we can to put our feet on land again."

Kiawak called to Tudlik, who used the chisel end of his harpoon to test the ice's strength.

To Elizapee's surprise, Poota and the two older men, with their knee-high sealskin boots, started kicking up water onto the ice beneath their feet until it was soaking wet. Then, with their mitted hands, they slid a large, rug-sized sheet of ice out of the water and shoved it carefully onto the wet ice between them. Then they kicked more water on top of it and hauled out a second large piece of ice and laid it on top of that. Now they had three ice sheets piled one on top of the other. This made the ice thicker than a human being lying on one side and, best of all, the water they had kicked on top was causing the ice to freeze together and stick like glue, making each layer stronger.

They continued splashing up water until another loose sheet of ice came and jammed against their small floe. They hauled it out, once more strengthening their thin floating island, working hard, like carpenters hurriedly building a floor. More drift ice struck their floe, and whenever a good-size piece of ice came near,

Kiawak and Tudlik lifted it out of the water. In a short time, they had more than thirty of these smaller pieces piled up near their strong ice floor.

Sharni, Elizapee, and Uvilu, wearing sealskin mitts, helped arrange these icy slabs.

Using the ice chisel, Tudlik began to cut and break each piece into rough squares about the size of a child's tabletop, and Kiawak and Poota stacked the squares together upright, leaning against each other to form a rough circle. Maylee, Sharni, and Uvilu gathered up soft, icy slush and melted it in their mouths. Then they spat it carefully between the new ice walls, like a kind of liquid glue.

"That should make them freeze together," Uvilu explained to Elizapee. "The wind is getting colder now. They will be frozen strong before dark."

The slush was so cold that it made Elizapee's teeth ache as she learned to do exactly what the other two girls were doing. Soon a squat ice igloo was rising upward. Finally, the men cleverly shaped and closed the dome of this strange, cold house.

Kiawak and Poota walked cautiously around their floating piece of ice, which Elizapee judged to be as large as a schoolroom. She thought their shelter was not much bigger than a round king-size bed she had once seen in a hotel room in the south. Poota tested the ice, taking wide steps like his father, as they clutched each other's wrists for safety. Before he took each step, Kiawak tested the ice with the sharp chisel end of his harpoon.

"Water went over the tops of my boots and my feet

are soaking wet," Uvilu told them, "but walking and working hard has warmed the water inside and my feet don't feel cold at all."

"You'll have to find a way to dry them before morning comes," said Sharni.

Elizapee looked around her at the ice-cold rippling of the windswept sea and shuddered in terror, for she could scarcely believe their floating island would hold together until morning came.

Tudlik froze the last, smallest pie-shaped slab of ice onto the domed top of their ice house, and Maylee was the first to move inside. She carried her stone lamp and tin of seal fat with her. Elizapee was trembling so hard that Maylee beckoned her to follow.

Outside, Uvilu and Sharni gathered their sleeping bags, caribou sleeping skins, and the four now-dried sealskins pulled from the bottom of the wrecked canoe.

"Here is a match," Maylee said to Elizapee. "It is damp, like everything else, but I think you can dry it by pulling back your parka hood and wiping it carefully in the driest part of your hair. While you're doing that, I'll prepare the lamp.

"I know you're as tired as I am," Maylee warned, "but do not sit or kneel on the ice. It will chill you to the bone. Do as I do. Squat down so only the soles of your boots touch the ice. That way your whole body will stay warmer."

Maylee propped her stone lamp on the ice.

"Try not to have your shadow block the light," Maylee said to Elizapee. "I need that last daylight coming through our ice wall to see what I am doing."

Maylee pulled one of her still-dry pant legs out of her boot, and with her *ulu* cut off a strip as wide as her finger. This dry piece she frayed and twisted in an expert way. As Elizapee watched her, Maylee dipped it into seal fat, which had partly melted. Then, with her *ulu* she tucked it neatly along the straight edge of her lamp, poured more seal oil over it, and placed chunks of soft seal fat in her lamp so that they would warm and melt into liquid, just like candle wax.

"*Ikumak piyumavunga,*" she said, and Elizapee handed her the match, for she had perfectly understood when Maylee said she wanted it.

"I could split this match in two if I had a razor blade," said Maylee in Inuktitut, but this time Elizapee only partly understood her words.

Maylee rubbed the match very gently in the softest inner fur of her parka, then struck it cautiously against the copper rivet that held the blade of her *ulu*. The match sputtered, faintly blue at first, and Elizapee was sure it would go out. But at last its center turned to orange, then yellow, as it caught and burst into flame.

Elizapee could hear Sharni and Uvilu outside the transparent house give a cry of relief when they saw the glow.

Maylee carefully sheltered the flame with her hand as she teased the fire expertly along the oily wick, causing a long line of light to rise raggedly from the edge of her lamp. Using her *ulu* handle, she tapped the wick until the flame was more than two hands long, burning high, with a warm and even light.

"That's a miracle!" Elizapee said as she held her freezing hands above the heat.

"Bring in the sealskins," Maylee called out to Uvilu and Sharni, "and then the sleeping bags."

Soon all seven of them were crammed into their small ice house. It felt wonderful to be in the light and out of the moaning, numbing wind.

"Let Lao come in, too," said Maylee.

"I'm glad that it's getting colder," Poota told Elizapee, "and that we have three layers of ice beneath us, because crowded together like this, we must be putting lots of weight on this floe. If we were on only one layer, we would surely melt it and plunge straight through."

"Don't talk like that," said Uvilu. "It makes me nervous. I don't like to think of all that freezing water flowing just beneath my feet."

"Neither do I," said Elizapee. "*Kapiashukunga*, I am afraid."

"So are we all," said Maylee, "but at least we're still alive."

"I'm glad we grabbed the sleeping bags," Elizapee told them, "but I wish I'd pulled out that leg of caribou."

"Well, no one can do everything at once," said Kiawak, "especially when everything is breaking all around you."

They held out their bare hands to gather welcome heat from the long white flame of the seal-oil lamp. Then, trying not to think of food, Maylee and Uvilu and Sharni expertly spread out the four waterproof sealskins, each with the hair side down, so that they would protect them from the wetness of the ice. They put torn pieces of canvas from the boat on top of the sealskins, then caribou skins hair-up beneath the sleeping bags, zipped open, which were on top. At last, they lay down, clinging closely to each other for warmth, and spread the third down-filled sleeping bag wide open like a blanket over all of them—except for Tudlik, who lay on one end with Lao close beside him. He said that she would keep him warm enough.

They were all grateful to be alive, and they snuggled close together before they fell asleep.

Only Elizapee remained awake. She could hear the change in the others' breathing, and she felt the deadly cold come seeping up from the ice beneath her, through the sealskin, the tattered bits of canvas, the caribou-skin sleeping robes, and through her clothing. I wonder why I am here, she asked herself again. Then raising her head, she looked at the peaceful, sleeping faces of Poota, Uvilu, and Sharni. Oh, yes, she knew why she was there. She could feel the warmth from everyone as she, too, closed her eyes and fell asleep.

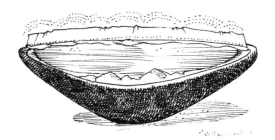

XII

THEY AWOKE IN THE MORNING, ALL SEVEN OF THEM still huddled together. Lao gave a low whine, meaning she was hungry. The heat from the lamp was almost gone and so was all but the last of the seal oil. Tudlik was the first up, the first to chip open the small frozen ice door and crawl outside. Lao followed him.

In a moment, he pushed Lao back inside and quietly told his daughter to hold her. Still on his hands and knees, he crept to his harpoon.

Elizapee watched through the entrance as Tudlik crawled to the edge of the ice and lay there without moving. Before long, a dark head came up out of the water, not far away. It seemed to be watching Sharni's father.

Tudlik cautiously raised himself in imitation of a basking seal, then slowly laid his head down on the ice. In his hunched position, with his dark parka and skin pants, Tudlik did look like a seal. The real seal rose up in the water, trying to get a better look at this familiar-looking creature lying on the ice. Then it ducked down out of sight.

Quickly, Tudlik felt inside his pocket and drew out his folding knife. He opened both blades and, reaching down, began to work the knife in the ice just at the water's edge.

"What's he doing?" Elizapee whispered to Uvilu, who was watching next to her.

"He's trying to sound like a seal's claws opening a breathing hole in the ice."

As Uvilu finished speaking, the seal's head came up not far from Tudlik. With a movement almost too fast to see, Tudlik cast his harpoon, sending it flying flat across the water. In an instant, he was on his feet and pulling hard on the harpoon line. He lunged back, then lay down, for the big male seal was dragging him across the ice. In a moment he would have to let go or be pulled into the water.

Sharni was the first outside and, falling on her belly, she slid across the ice, catching her father by his parka hood. Poota was right after her and, kneeling, pulled with all his might, drawing them away from the dangerous edge of the ice.

The seal dove and struggled hard, but its life's strength was running out. Soon it was floating quietly in the water, and Tudlik carefully hauled in the harpoon line, coiling it neatly until he could reach down and catch hold of the seal's flipper. Gratefully, he and Poota drew this plump, life-giving treasure up out of the water and onto the ice. This big male seal had come to them and given its life so that they might go on living, for a while at least.

It was Maylee and the three girls who cut up the seal, saving every part of it: its hide for warmth, its fat for burning in the lamp, its flesh for eating, its sinews for sewing, and even its meaty bones, some of which they gave to Lao.

While they did this, Poota, his father, and Tudlik took up places on three corners of their floating home, their harpoons ready, each one hoping for another seal.

It was just as cold and windy as the day before, but at least the autumn sun had climbed above the mist and the sky was blue above them. Far to the north, they could see a thin white line of ice, and beyond that the snow-crested mountains on the mainland.

"If only this wind would change," said Poota when he came inside their crude igloo to warm himself at the lamp, which now burned brightly with the new seal oil.

Suddenly they heard Kiawak yell, for he had harpooned another seal. Poota ran outside and helped his father in the struggle until the seal's spirit left its body. Only then were they able to pull it up onto the ice.

Before night spread its darkness over their moving island, Poota had taken his first seal, and Tudlik had harpooned another one as well.

"Four in one day!" said Poota's father. "The sea goddess must be trying to help us. Now if this north wind will only turn around, and blow us to the land."

They all ate their fill of food that night, and it made them feel much warmer. In the morning when Elizapee went outside, the air was almost warm, and the weather fine and still. The sea around them lay as smooth as glass, reflecting the sky like a giant mirror.

"Why are we still moving?" Elizapee asked Kiawak, as the others stretched and dried the sealskins.

"Because of the strength of the tide. It's still carrying us eastward, far away from the land."

No seals came near them that day, and not long after noon, the sun formed a small blue pool of water on top of the ice. Poota splashed it with his foot.

"We don't want too much warming," he said. "That could ruin this ice boat of ours."

Elizapee scarcely slept at all that night as she imagined their island melting beneath them.

In the morning, there was no wind and the weather seemed even warmer. But the seals were back again. Looking out over the calm water, Elizapee could see the heads of half a dozen of them. The three hunters took up their places by the edge of the ice.

Elizapee was inside the ice house, making thread, combing and separating seal sinew in the way that Maylee had shown her, when she felt the ice tremble and she heard Poota's father yell.

"The ice is breaking! Get out of that igloo!"

As Elizapee scrambled out in terror, she saw Poota, carrying his harpoon, make a desperate run, then leap across some open water onto their part of the floating ice. Poota walked steadily toward her.

The seven of them stood and watched in horror as

the larger, thinner part of their ice island drifted away.

"The sun and tide did that," said Tudlik. "We have to do something. We can't just sit here and wait. What can we do?"

On this day, the curiosity of the seals seemed to bring them even closer around their piece of ice. By midday, the hunters had harpooned three more. Two of them were big ones. Maylee and the girls swiftly cut them up, carefully saving the skins.

When Kiawak brought in the fourth seal, it was almost growing dark. He and Poota watched a small, red-footed seabird paddling hard against the power of the outflowing tide.

Poota examined the wreckage of their canoe, which lay scattered on the ice. Tudlik and Kiawak squatted down beside the longest wooden length of keel.

"We might make something with this," said Kiawak.

Tudlik looked at him. "Have you ever built a kayak?"

"No," said Kiawak, "but I saw my grandfather and my uncle build one when I was very young."

"Let's start now," Tudlik said to Kiawak. "Poota will help us and the women will prepare the skins. I don't believe this small piece of ice we're riding on will last more than a day or two, and this tide is sweeping us eastward toward the ocean."

They had no plan, no drawing for building a kayak, only a kind of dream, a memory inside each of the hunters' heads. First, using sealskin strips, the two men bound the three broken pieces of the keel to-gether while Poota searched in the darkness for every single piece of broken canoe rib he could find. For a while, it seemed useless to him, for he knew he would never find half enough. "We will not be able to do what we are trying to do," he muttered to himself.

"How can we make a kayak," he asked Tudlik, "if we've got almost nothing here?"

"Hurry, quickly," Tudlik answered, "unless you can teach all these people to fly!"

Kiawak, Tudlik, and Poota worked through the moonless early winter night, welcoming the northern lights when they appeared above their heads. Elizapee came out once and looked up. It was as though some ghostly images were dancing, prancing high above them in the sky.

When dawn came, the framework of their new kayak was nearly finished. It looked almost laughable to all of them, far too weak to hold a single person. It needed ribs for strength and there were no more wooden ribs, only a few shredded pieces of canvas.

"My father told me," Tudlik said, "that at least one seal rib was usually built into every kayak to prove to the seals that the hunter needs them and respects them."

"That's it!" said Poota. "That's what we can use— these seal ribs! Forget wooden ribs, we've got lots of bone!"

"Good," said Kiawak. "Let's try it."

By drilling each rib on both sides with the small steel drill from the outboard engine kit that had been tied inside the stern of the canoe, the hunters found that they could lash these seal ribs into place to strengthen their long kayak. They worked hard almost all that day and night.

As soon as dawn arrived the following morning, Maylee went out to check their efforts on the kayak. "I did not believe you could build a kayak out of almost nothing. The girls have resoaked the skins and are starting to sew them. But we will need at least one more."

All that day, the hunters watched the sea around them. But not a single seal appeared.

Maylee and the girls had many of the skins sewn together, using seal back sinews as thread. They were able to cover the kayak except for one piece on the front deck.

"You can use these," said Elizapee as she undid the string and stepped out of her outer pants.

"If the wind comes up, you'll freeze out here with only those blue jeans on," said Sharni.

"I've got my thick pajamas underneath," Elizapee told her.

Maylee smiled at Elizapee, as she quickly slit the pants open.

Working together, the girls fitted and sewed in Elizapee's sealskin pants. They were the last piece needed to complete the kayak's skin.

They propped up the new kayak on two ice blocks, then tied it down safely, using the canoe line. All that day, a drying wind blew to them from the south, and by sunup on the following day, the kayak's skin had shrunk to drumhead tightness. When the morning mists cleared, they found themselves much closer to the strong land-ice around Baffin Island. But even as they watched, the huge tide started forcing them east again, east toward the dreaded ocean and the big, fast-moving fields of crushing ice.

XIII

"I HOPE THE OLD WOODEN RIBS AND THE NEW SEAL ones are strong enough to hold this rough kayak together," Kiawak said.

"Will our sinew sewing, done so quickly, hold well enough to keep the water out?" asked Maylee with a worried look.

Poota was proud of the kayak, for it was the first he had ever helped to build. They stood the long, slender craft on its end and shook it to test its strength. Elizapee's pants still looked like Elizapee's pants, now well-sewn into the front deck of the kayak. Would the pants bring them luck? Lao sniffed the new sealskin kayak, as if she, too, were wondering if this pack of skins and bones would take them anywhere.

"Let me be the first to try it," Poota said.

"You've got a lot of courage, just like your grandfather," Kiawak answered, as he and Tudlik lowered the kayak carefully into the water.

Poota eased himself down through the round hole in the upper deck, and Tudlik handed him the double-bladed paddle that he had made from the two cracked paddle blades. He had repaired them and then bound them tightly at each end of his harpoon shaft. Cautiously, Poota stroked away from the ice, then toured once around their floating island.

"Now let us see if this kayak will take the weight of others," Tudlik said.

"Let's try it," Poota answered.

He got out and helped his mother squeeze head first underneath the front deck. To balance the weight, Poota put some seal meat and her lamp and pot under the back deck before getting in again.

"I'd like to have somebody lie on the back deck," Poota said. "That way we can test it better."

Sharni stepped forward and carefully crawled on top of the back deck of the kayak. It sank dangerously low in the water. Poota took out some of the heavier pieces of meat until the kayak seemed to balance.

"I'll try to paddle over to the main ice and then hurry back for the rest of you."

"Good luck," Elizapee called, as Poota gently pushed the kayak away from the ice and took his first strokes. "Oh, I'm afraid even to watch them," Elizapee whispered to Uvilu as she turned her head away. "That kayak is so low in the water I can hardly see it."

The light wind and the tide seemed to help the dangerously loaded craft, but it took a long time before Sharni and Poota were able to climb safely onto the shore ice surrounding Baffin Island, then carefully help Maylee out. She pulled her lamp and the seal meat with her. The solid, snow-covered winter ice so firmly attached to the shore of the large island felt thick and strong beneath their feet.

"Your arms must be very tired," Maylee said. "You should wait and rest."

"No, I'm all right," said Poota. "I'm leaving now."

He climbed once more into the empty kayak, and, stroking as manfully as he could, he returned through the dangerous fields of moving ice to the floating island where his father, Elizapee, Uvilu, and Tudlik were waiting for him.

"It's my turn to do some work," Kiawak said. "You stay here and get some rest. I'll take Uvilu up inside the front with some meat and Tudlik will lie on the back. I'll paddle," Kiawak told them.

Just as Kiawak started to push off, Lao jumped lightly from the ice onto the kayak's front deck and lay down.

"Can you do that?" Poota asked his father. "Can you take her, too?"

"If she doesn't move around," said Kiawak, but for the first time he could feel the great weight on the kayak and hear its rib bones straining and its wooden framework creak. He started cautiously toward the main ice where Maylee and Sharni were standing, looking as small as young sea ducks.

"Are you all right?" Kiawak asked his passengers.

"*Ajii*," said Tudlik. "Yes."

"*Ajii*," answered Uvilu.

"Good. Everyone stay steady. You, too, Lao."

"I can't believe how low in the water they are," Elizapee said to Poota. "Do you think they'll ever get there . . . then back here again?"

"I hope they will," Poota answered, and they looked at each other with silent fear secretly spreading inside each of them.

"With no load, it was easy to paddle back here," Poota told Elizapee. "Tudlik's strong. He'll come back and paddle us across. But I don't like the way the wind is changing."

"I'm glad you're the one to be here with me," Elizapee told him. "I'd be terrified, if I were drifting out here . . . alone."

"Well, you're not alone, and I hope you'll never be alone," said Poota. "You'll always be part of our family."

"That makes me feel wonderful," said Elizapee, shading her eyes. "Look, the kayak's coming back for us."

The two of them worked together, rolling the sleeping bags tight and gathering the remaining meat, ready to stuff it all inside the kayak.

Tudlik got out and stretched his powerful arms, then held the kayak steady as Elizapee crawled under the forward deck before he got back in. Poota stretched out flat on top of the back deck. Tudlik turned his head and took one last look at the old-fashioned ice house they had built to save their lives. The wind was coming dead against them now, and their house was sagging inward.

Poota felt fear rising in him as he laid his head on

the back sealskin deck. He could hear the wood and seal bones creaking and groaning.

A few minutes later, Elizapee called out, "There's quite a lot of water coming through the bottom. I'm getting very wet in here."

Poota could hear Tudlik grunting, straining with each stroke, trying desperately to save their lives.

"Elizapee, are you all right?" Poota called to her.

There was no answer.

"Elizapee! Elizapee!" he called again.

"*Tukungilanga,*" she cried back. "I'm not dead. I'm trying to hold my head up out of the water."

Poota could see Tudlik's wide back slumping forward, his great arms going slower and slower.

"Hand me back the paddle and you rest," Poota demanded, and from his awkward position lying on the back deck, he paddled as hard as he could toward the others who stood helplessly on the ice watching the terrible struggle. He could hear the kayak's ribs cracking and water sloshing inside.

"Give me back the paddle," Tudlik gasped. "My strength is coming back to me."

With long, slow, mighty strokes, he drove the kayak's bow straight toward Kiawak and Sharni, who were kneeling at the edge of the ice waiting. The instant they could grab the slender bow, with the help of Uvilu and Maylee, they dragged the whole sinking kayak straight up onto the ice.

Tudlik flung himself out of the cockpit of the kayak and lay gasping on the snow. "Get her out of there . . . Get Elizapee out!" he shouted.

Poota and Sharni each caught Elizapee by one foot and dragged her out.

Elizapee was soaking wet and shuddering and sobbing, but the first words she said were, "Don't worry, I'm okay. I'm alive!"

"We've got them all," said Tudlik. "We're all here on the main ice together again. Alive!"

Slowly, gratefully, Kiawak pulled out the seal meat and the soaked sleeping bags. Poota saw that the kayak's deck was now torn and hanging sideways, and the kayak itself was bent in the middle, where most of the ribs had been broken. He and his father rolled it over, dumping the water out of it.

"We built a snowhouse here while you were gone," said Maylee. "All of you get inside right now. You're soaking wet. I've got the lamp burning in there and we'll rub you down and lend you some of our drier clothes."

"What a day this has been," said Tudlik, trying to move his arms. "I've never felt so tired, or so glad to have my feet on solid ice."

"I've made a little porch to protect the meat," said Kiawak. "We will eat first, then sleep. Tomorrow we can decide what will be best for us to do."

Poota was the last to wake the next morning to the smell of seal meat boiling over the family's lamp. His mother had somehow stayed awake all night to turn and dry their boots and clothing. When he was finished eating, Poota bent double to ease out through the igloo's entrance tunnel.

Outside, Tudlik was squatting on the snow beside

the ruins of the kayak. Kiawak was cutting away the sealskins.

Poota heard Elizapee say to his father in clear Inuktitut, *"Kadlit piyumavunga iluwak."* Then, smiling, Kiawak handed Elizapee her sealskin pants that had been cut open and sewn into the kayak's deck.

"Nakoamiasit," she said. "Thanks a lot."

"I'm glad to hear you're getting good at the language," Kiawak told her.

Poota helped Kiawak and Tudlik and in no time they had finished cutting the kayak apart. Using the long wooden keel and upper rims of the canoe's wooden frame, they began to rebuild the kayak into a narrow sled, using the wood and the seal ribs and bones for crossbars. They lashed and bound them together, binding them with the sinews and lashings that had once secured their kayak.

"I would never ever have imagined building a broken canoe into a kayak and then into a sled like that," Elizapee told Poota as they helped load their precious, tightly rolled sleeping bags, the lamp, the pot, and a heavy bundle of seal meat onto the new-formed sled, then lashed them firmly into place. "We should have Inuit teachers in our schools down south to teach us such marvelous survival tricks."

"Roll and tie the kayak skins," Maylee told the girls as she finished sewing Elizapee's outer sealskin pants together again. "We'll sleep on those skins tonight."

They harnessed Lao to the sled and everyone held across one shoulder a separate sealskin line attached to the sled. Acting together like a team, they fanned out and began to pull. Heading eastward, they hoped they would find other nomad families who would help them.

They did not talk or sing, but walked in silence, each wondering what had happened to the others in the white boat after they had last seen it so many days ago. Elizapee, like the others, had forgotten the number of days.

That night, they moved off the sea ice and onto the safety of Baffin's land once more. They built their igloo in a long, hard snowdrift and they all ate as much rich seal meat as they could hold. Their snowhouse was large enough this time for all of them to lie in comfort. And with the kayak cover under them, they were better able to arrange the now-dried sleeping bags so that, for the first night since they had been crushed in the ice, they were able to sleep comfortably together.

Next morning, they left the igloo early, helping Lao pull their curious sled. It grew cold and windy during the brief midday.

As night was falling, Lao stopped, turned her head, and sniffed the breeze. When they tried to go forward, she refused and instead let out a low howl and sat down.

"Be careful," said Poota. "She sometimes does that when she senses wolves are hunting nearby."

But this time Lao only wanted to change direction. She wanted to lead all of them onto a long, ice-covered fjord lying between the mountains.

"We should follow her," said Uvilu. "She has some special reason to go that way."

Tail down and pulling hard, Lao struggled to go up the fjord.

"We will follow her for a while," said Kiawak. "She seems to be trying to tell us something, but I don't think there are hunters living near this fjord."

They had not gone far when Lao sat down again, tipped back her head, and gave a long howl. The seven humans stopped, remaining motionless while they listened. Far ahead of them, they heard an answering howl. Lao jumped up and started pulling strongly forward once more.

"Was that a dog howling?" Sharni asked her father. "Someone could be living up there."

"It sounded like a wolf to me," said Uvilu.

Elizapee felt fear at the very sound of the Inuktitut word *amarok*, which meant "wolf." A half moon cast its light across the mountains, making the snow glow in an eerie way. The northern lights were beaming now above their heads, moving like ghostly airport searchlights cutting through the darkness.

Elizapee heard the howling of the wolves again much closer, and she shuddered as the icy fingers of the night wind moved up beneath her parka, her shirt, and her pajama top, along her trembling spine.

XIV

"LISTEN CAREFULLY," KIAWAK CALLED TO THE OTH-
ers. "I believe those are sled dogs howling. And
they're not far away."

Lao answered with another howl, and they all pulled
together toward the sound.

"Can you see them?" Uvilu asked Elizapee.

There before her were five pale, frosted windows,
faintly glowing in the darkness. Then orange lights
appeared as small square doors were flung open.

They could hear the sound of human voices.
Quickly, they dragged their sled up the bank toward
the camp, then stopped in amazement.

There among the snowy shadows on the fjord's
beach stood *Oopik*, the white boat. Tudlik and his
daughter, Sharni, dropped their pulling lines and ran
toward their family boat. It had not been thrown there
by a storm. It was not smashed or broken by the ice.

Two boys came running through the dark toward

them and they could see the silhouette of a man and woman against the patches of light.

"Who are you?" Tudlik called out cautiously, for he could now see a dozen dark shadows running toward them.

"Who are you?" the fjord people called back, perhaps worried themselves that these creatures were not human, but some spirits from beneath the sea. No one could be sure who might be traveling in these lonely mountain fjords.

"We are Nesarmiut, the hat-island people," Tudlik shouted. "Who are you?"

"Ohhh, husband!" cried Nepeesha, as she ran to him. "And you, too, dear Sharni! We have been so afraid for all of you."

"We are all of us alive and well," called Kiawak.

"*Ajii*," Sharni called out. "All seven of us have returned."

They heard other men's and women's voices, and many people, young and old, began to gather around to greet them. They were all friends they knew well from another hunting camp of nomad families.

"We're all right. Every one of us is safe," cried old Paar, who was standing in the doorway of a winter tent. "We Nesarmiut are once more together."

"How did you get here?" Kiawak asked them.

"We pushed the white boat," answered Parr. "We skidded it along the ice until we arrived at this camp."

Young Emik, who was standing beside his grandfather, ran to his family.

Elizapee watched the three male dogs in this new camp start to circle Lao as she was unharnessed. The girls carried their sleeping bags inside the winter tents and the hunters put the last of their food supply into the safety of a stone meat cache.

"Oh, Elizapee! Look who's living with the families here!" Sharni cried out with pleasure, as did Uvilu and Poota. "It's Tomasi, our teacher who moves around a lot. He's visiting this camp."

Tomasi was rugged and strong-looking, with bright dark eyes and wide cheekbones. His white teeth flashed when he smiled. He was living with the Pumiuk family. Everyone shook hands with the seven newcomers.

When they had settled down with mugs of tea inside Pumiuk's winter tent, Tomasi talked to Elizapee. "It's not hard being an itinerant teacher around here. Look at the good students I've got, like all of these."

He spoke to Elizapee in Inuktitut, but she answered him in English.

"I'm new to these camps, but I'm eager to take lessons if I'm going to live out at Nesak Island this winter. I can't go on missing school forever."

"Oh, we'll fix that," Tomasi said encouragingly. "I've got some extra books and test papers on the snowmobile. I'll give you everything you'll need for your grade level."

"I don't know why Elizapee is speaking English to you," Maylee said. "She speaks Inuktitut very well now. She's a part of our camp."

These were her people, Elizapee knew. She was part of their nomad way of life, but no one here recognized her.

"When are you coming back to Nesak to check our

lessons and teach us new ideas?" asked Sharni, for she seemed to have a special interest in Tomasi.

"Stay with us as long as you wish," said Pumiuk, who was the strongest hunter in this camp. "Live in our tents with us. Then, when you are rested and feel ready, we will gladly take you on our snowmobiles into Frobisher Bay. You Nesak Island people, having skidded your white boat all this way to us, are welcome to leave it here until the summer seas are open. Then come back and visit us before you take it back home to your island."

Tomasi looked at Sharni, then at Elizapee and Uvilu. "This must have been a long, hard journey for all of you," he said. "Do you feel strong enough to go on to Frobisher with Poota and me on my snowmobile? I'll be pulling a short sled. Or, you could stay here with old Paar, Poota's grandfather, and a few of the other women until we get back."

"I wouldn't want you to go without me," said Elizapee.

"Then we'll leave three days from now in the early morning, if the weather's good. You look thin like all the others," Tomasi told Elizapee. "Eat a lot to make you strong again. Sharni's mother says your warm caribou pants and parka—the ones you helped make—are with all the other winter clothing stored inside the boat."

"It's going to be a long, cold ride," Poota warned, "but it's got to be better than our last trip when we broke up that canoe!" He smiled at Elizapee and then at Sharni.

On the morning when they left, the weather was

clear and all those going were ready. Poota was certainly right about it being cold on the snowmobiles all that day.

They spent the first night of their journey to Frobisher Bay in a mountain valley where there was no wind. The whole sky had been blown clear and bright stars were coming out. The young people worked together and swiftly built an igloo, made tea inside, and shared hot food. Later, the other Nesak Island people arrived and built their own snowhouses a few paces away.

When the young people were alone in their snowhouse, they looked up in wonder at the millions of crystals in the igloo's dome, twinkling in the candlelight above their heads. Sharni said, "Tomasi, tell Elizapee what it is like to be an itinerant teacher."

"I travel around, working, teaching," Tomasi told them. "But I think it's just as good as being an ordinary teacher. At least I like it a lot."

"Why?"

"Because I travel. I'm always visiting different groups of students as I move around among the four camps that I work with. Just when Sharni, Uvilu, Poota, Nuna, and the other students are wanting to do something else, like fishing, hunting, dancing, and learning from their fathers to build igloos and from their mothers to sew, I leave them with further lessons and move on. That way, they can learn all the special Inuit things they need to know and study the lessons I leave with them as well. Then I visit another camp with other Inuit students. When I get back to my friends here about two moons later, I check their lessons and their papers to see how well they've studied while I was away."

"Do you like it as well as going to an ordinary school in one of the larger settlements?" Elizapee asked Uvilu and Poota.

"We both like it a lot better," Poota answered.

"Most families here have lived for a while in one of those larger settlements just so their kids could go to school," said Uvilu, "and so we'd all be close to the nursing station, which makes it really simple for the nurse to check our health. Being close to the school made it easy for a regular teacher to teach us. After all, that's the way they do it in the south."

"Well, what's wrong with that?" Elizapee asked.

"Everything," Tomasi and Poota and Sharni answered together.

"This isn't the south," Tomasi continued. "Poota and Uvilu's father, Kiawak, and Sharni's father, Tudlik, they're both hunters. Nomads like Kiawak and Tudlik and their wives have taken care of their Inuit families and helped their neighbors for thousands of years. They've learned to live a life where they can stay close with one another and enjoy the land and sea and sky and stars, stay close to the animals, birds, and fish, but especially close to their own families, the relatives they love.

"For a while after World War II, the people in the government didn't know what they were going to do about Inuit living in the Arctic. Then, slowly at first, they started bringing nomad Inuit families into the settlements to make it easier for the southern nurses and teachers to help and teach them. They probably thought that their kind of southern schooling, and the southern style of living, would work well for Inuit-Eskimos everywhere. But mostly it has not. Over in Greenland, we have heard that they are now trying hard to provide Inuit education in a very different way, the itinerant way. I'm helped to the same thing around here as a kind of experiment," said Tomasi. "I think you're being taught by both family and school in a way that really gives you a choice of how you're later going to live your lives, either here in the north or maybe in the south. You could be a hunter, a carver, a pilot or a teacher, a doctor or a nurse, perhaps a carpenter, a bulldozer driver, or a computer expert.

"Well, you'll be at the end of Frobisher Bay tomorrow, Elizapee. There's a big town there called Iqaluit, and you will be able to judge all this for yourself."

When they were finished eating, they carefully spread two white bear skins down and three caribou skins hair up. Then they unrolled their separate sleeping bags on top.

"It will be really cold tonight when the heat seeps out of this igloo," Uvilu said as they lay down.

XV

THE NEXT MORNING VERY EARLY, POOTA WENT OUT to check the weather, then came back inside the igloo. He squatted down, pumped up their small brass Primus stove, and pulled his mitt down out of the nose hole that he had carved the night before in the dome of the igloo to let out the gases of the stove when it was going, but had plugged again when they were sleeping.

Tomasi raised his head, looked at Poota, and then at his wristwatch. "What's keeping you from getting back in your sleeping bag?" he asked.

"There's a bad storm building in the mountains west of here. You can see the clouds breaking into pieces as they touch the peaks, and there's a huge drift of falling snow behind them."

Tomasi sat up, pulled on a heavy sweater, then climbed out of his sleeping bag. His long winter underwear looked white and very new.

Poota reached back and shook his sister, Uvilu, then Elizapee and Sharni. "Tomasi and I are getting ready to go now," he told them as he put the kettle full of ice on the burner to make the tea. "There's a mountain storm blowing out of the west and we are sleeping in its path. We don't want to be caught and held here for several days. If we hurry down the mountain now and reach sea level, we should escape to Frobisher Bay without much trouble. But we've got to move right now."

Tomasi woke the others in their igloos.

While still inside her sleeping bag, Sharni pulled on her skin pants and parka top, then stretched and smiled at Tomasi. "Don't look at your watch. I could have used more sleep."

She opened her backpack and took out a round, pie-sized bannock thicker than her hand. "Elizapee, will you cut this into five even pieces for us with that fancy new *ulu* that somebody gave you?"

Elizapee smiled as she hunted for the moon-shaped blade, then glanced at Poota as she started carefully cutting. Uvilu threw a handful of tea into the kettle as the steam rose and spread a fog above their heads inside the snowy igloo dome.

Elizapee was amazed at how quickly these, her own people, working together, could build a strong snow shelter for the night, then break camp in the morning and be off. Elizapee had tented often on the southern lakes. But unpacking, setting up their camp, then later repacking into a station wagon had seemed a slow and endless task. These Inuit of hers were experts at moving, and they swiftly lashed their loads onto the sled.

Jumping onto the snowmobile and the sled it pulled, they went down the mountainside together. Always these northern people were watchful and cautious, for they intended to continue surviving in nature as they had for countless generations.

When the snowmobile reached the level of the lowest hills above the shore, Uvilu nudged Elizapee and pointed. "It's still too gray to see it yet, but Iqaluit is right over there across the bay."

"Look up, look back," called Tomasi. "The mountain where we slept has disappeared inside the storm that Poota was the first to see."

Sharni pulled back Tomasi's sleeve and looked at his watch. "It's only ten minutes before eight," she told Elizapee. "Can you believe that the worst part of our journey is over?"

"I loved coming down that mountainside." Elizapee laughed. "I've never had a ride like that before."

When they were halfway across the flat ice of the snow-covered bay, they could see the gray outline of the tallest government building, then the school and the airport tower and a scattering of smaller houses, their bright colors shining in the early morning light.

"It looks like good weather over there," Poota said.

"I haven't been to Iqaluit for more than two years," Uvilu told Elizapee. "There are always lots of new things to see in Iqaluit. Plenty of exciting things are always happening there."

"I've been there before," Elizapee said. "My family wasn't there."

They went up through the jagged tidal ice and entered Iqaluit on a rough snow track. When they reached the first crossroad, they stopped.

Elizapee, Uvilu, Poota, Tomasi, and Sharni stood together like strangers, nomads huddled beside Tomasi's long snowmobile and sled, staring at the one huge four-engine plane and one smaller red helicopter resting on the Arctic airstrip not far from the yellow airport tower. Then they looked up at the snow road leading to the office buildings, and the school with the hospital high behind it, then rows and rows of government houses.

"Don't expect Inuit or *kadlunait*—white people from the south—to come rushing out to greet you here," Uvilu told Elizapee. "This is such a huge place that they don't even know when their cousins from the camps arrive. Where would you like to go first?"

"I don't know," Elizapee said. "You all choose."

"There's an inn over there that sells food. We could go and eat," said Tomasi. "But there's only one small light in the back. I guess it's not open yet."

"I'm not too hungry yet," said Sharni, and Elizapee agreed.

"We could go and visit our aunt and cousins." Uvilu waved her mitt. "They live up on Apex Hill."

"Let's do that," said Tomasi. "I've got two good friends up there I want to see. Their names are Kayak and Mattoosie. They got lost once out beyond those mountains, and they met a wild man, and a polar bear that saved their lives. They found a lot of gold, but threw it all away. They live here now. I want to see what those two are up to."

All five of them jumped back onto Tomasi's snowmobile and sled as he started up the hard-packed snow
road. They passed the school. It was round-shaped,
like a huge upside-down metal pot, with a bright red
line that zigzagged all around it.

"Tomasi, would you like to be a teacher in that
school?" Poota shouted over the noise of the snowmobile.

"It might be all right, but I'm happy doing what I
do." He smiled as he rounded the curve. "Here we
are on Apex Hill."

Even the tiny village of Apex looked big to them,
with many small, brightly painted Inuit houses. Tomasi
stopped his snowmobile in front of the cousins' house.
Uvilu opened the unlocked door of the house.

"*Eteri!* Come in!" a voice called to them. It was their
cousin, Neevee, eating breakfast with her brother,
Pilipusi. "Oh, Uvilu, Poota! You're all just in time for
breakfast. Take off your parkas. Sit down at the table.
Who are these three new people with you?"

"She's Elizapee, who lives with us, and he's Tomasi,
our itinerant teacher who travels everywhere, and
she's Sharni," Uvilu answered. "You must know her
family."

Then all shook hands with the cousins.

Tomasi spoke to Sharni. "I'm going to visit my two
friends now. Do you want to come with me?"

Sharni agreed. "We'll come back later," she said as
they went outside and quickly closed the door.

"Elizapee has had a very strange life," Uvilu told
her cousin. "Let her tell you after breakfast."

"It will have to wait until after school," said Neevee,

looking at the alarm clock sitting by the sink. "The school bus will be here for us in about three minutes."

"You people in Apex really do live by the clocks," said Poota. "That's why we Nesak Islanders like living in the camps."

Uvilu's two cousins, Neevee and Pilipusi, gobbled down their breakfast, then bundled into their outer clothing.

As they were about to leave, Poota called, "Wait! I'm coming with you. I've got some friends inside that big silver building that you Iqalummiut call a school."

While Elizapee and Uvilu were finishing a much slower breakfast, Uvilu pulled off her sweater. "These cousins of mine keep it dripping hot inside this house, and when they visit our camps, they say they're always cold. Do you feel hot?" she asked Elizapee.

"Yes. I'm nearly roasted. This is the way they used to keep the hospitals and houses down south."

"We used to like cold houses, too," Uvilu's uncle said as he came out of the bedroom and shook hands. "But now we've changed. Everything here is changing very fast for us." He looked out through a small clearing in one of the frosted windowpanes.

"I still don't like a house too hot," said Kopiniwak, the grandmother, who had also come in, as she poured herself a cup of tea. She began to weave a woolen belt.

"Are there many older people in Iqaluit?" Elizapee asked the grandmother in Inuktitut.

"*Ajii*, quite a few."

"Were they all born around here?"

"No. Most of them came from other places. There

were some small camps along the coast of this big island and on the inland fjords. That's where most folks here were born. They came to live in this place when the air force came and afterward stayed because they wanted to. That was before the government said their children had to go to school."

"That's the way they do it in the south," Elizapee said. "When families want to stay some place, they stay. When they want to go or have to move, they take their children with them. Most kids can find schools almost anywhere in North America."

"Why can't we do that?" the grandmother asked the girls. "I used to like it so much better living out in a camp with my husband and our children and all our relatives nearby us. Now I don't know half the people living around me. Most are from some place far up north or west of here."

"I'd like to talk to some of these older people," Elizapee said. "Maybe there's someone here who knows or remembers my family."

The old woman stared at Elizapee for some time. "You could go and see Sala. She's the oldest woman around here. Sala's got a lovely memory," the grandmother continued. "She might not remember what she had for breakfast this morning, but the great thing is she can remember every single thing that happened long ago, even when she was a small girl much younger than you."

"Where does Sala live?" Uvilu asked. "I'd like to take Elizapee to visit her."

"Well, that's not so easy as it sounds. She lives up

in a kind of sky house her son made for her. It's built a bit like that tower at the airport where the *kadlunait* call to the airplanes each day, even through the fog. When I tried to climb those shelflike stairs of hers, she had to help me with a rope. I couldn't do it by myself. She invited me up to see it once, which is a lot more than she does for most folks. Sala doesn't like all the hustling and bustling that goes on around here. She's like me, she likes the outdoor life, moving on the land.

"We drank tea together and talked and talked. It was more than worth the trip for me. I could see for the first time why Sala wanted to be up so high. She likes to sit at her big window. On a clear day, she can see right across the bay to those far mountains running south to the edge of Silveea. That's her glacier. Sala was born down there. It doesn't so much matter when a person was born," the grandmother said, "but where and why they were born . . . that's the main question."

Elizapee sighed. "That's just exactly what I'm trying to find out. Who am I? Who were my parents? Where was the place that I was born?"

"I can't help you, but I wouldn't be surprised if Sala could."

"I know a shortcut to that tall house of hers on the back hill," said Uvilu. "I'll take Elizapee there right now."

"Good," said the grandmother, and she smiled at both the girls. "Say hello to Sala for me. You should get there before midday, because after that she does her exercises. You know, jumping up and down and swinging her arms like a bird that's learning to fly."

The two girls ran down the snow road to Sala's house. It was really more like two separate houses joined together, one low, the other thin and high. Uvilu knocked on the door of the low house.

No one answered. Uvilu opened the door and called, "Anybody home?"

No answer.

"Let's go around to the tower-house door," Elizapee said. But when they knocked there, there was still no answer.

"Is it locked?" asked Uvilu.

Elizapee tried the knob, then gently pushed to open the door.

"Thank you for sending up that breath of clear, fresh air," a quavering voice called down to them. "The only time I usually get a whiff of it is about eight in the morning and again at half past five when my son and his wife get home from work. Who are you two?"

"I'm Uvilu," Uvilu called up the strange-shaped stairs, which looked far more like a school library's bookshelves than like real stairs. "My great-aunt, Kopiniwak, sent us here. I've got my best friend, Elizapee, with me. She wants to talk to you."

"Well, not today, girls. This is my hideaway. I'm getting kind of old and I don't let just anyone come up here poking around among my treasures, because they go away and tell people. Then others come here with their friends, all knocking on my door, expecting me to do some ancient kind of remembering for them. So good-bye, girls."

"Wait! Wait!" Elizapee called up to her. "I'm here because I don't know my own name or who my parents are or where I came from. I was told you might try to help me."

"Oh, here we go again. Well, if only one of you comes up, I guess it won't bother me too much. This place is small and I don't take to crowds."

"Then Elizapee is coming alone," called Uvilu. "I'll give her some help from behind to start her up these unusual stairs of yours."

"Oh, she can't get up with just a bottom boost from you," the old woman called down. "I'll have to unreel the long rope for her. Together, we can hoist her up."

The long rope came slithering down the bookshelf stairs. Elizapee caught its end, which had two hand knots, and started scrambling upward, with Uvilu pushing her from behind. Twisting and turning as she climbed, she clung like a monkey to the rope.

"Whew! Reeling you up is heavy work!" said the old woman as Elizapee's head appeared. She caught hold of her arms and pulled her to safety.

"My name's Sala and I don't know why, but somehow you look kind of familiar to me."

"I'm glad I look familiar to somebody," Elizapee said. "I really believe no one in this whole world remembers me."

"Well, I don't really remember you," said Sala. "What's your name?"

"Elizabeth Queen," she answered, "but Inuit in the camps call me Elizapee." Then, turning, she looked all around. "Oh, my! What a magical-looking house! I've never seen a place like this before."

"Well, I've been told there are no others like it," the old woman said with pride. "The main thing up here that is interesting is for you to sit right down in my chair and have a good look through my grandfather's bring-near glass. Be careful. Don't touch it or I'll have to ask my son to set it clear and bright again.

"My grandfather, Pootagook was his name, went out with the Scots and the Americans when they used to sail around here hunting whales. My grandfather was a famous harpooneer. One year he was out in his kayak and he caught an *adlanguak*. Those sailors called them sea unicorns. Did you ever see one? Each male has one long, twisted ivory horn sticking straight out front. My grandfather told me that tusk he got stood much taller than himself. A whaling captain wanted to have that ivory sea-unicorn horn so much that he traded my grandfather this treasure—his own long, shiny, brass bring-near glass—just for that one tusk. Sila, she's the spirit woman who controls the wind and sky, she made the weather clear today, so if you look carefully, you can just see my big glacier, Silveea, shining in the sun down Frobisher Bay."

"That glacier looks like a huge birthday cake," said Elizapee.

"You're lucky to see it now," said Sala.

"It's wonderful," said Elizapee, easing herself out of Sala's armchair, careful not to shake the telescope. "What are these?" Elizapee asked, pointing to a table.

"The great bone eardrums from a whale. My grandfather gave them to me. If you listen inside them, you can sometimes hear a high, sweet sound. A young lad from Scotland visited me here. He said it sounded like his tape recordings of the underwater calling of the whales. But I believe he's got that wrong. I think it's the singing of Taluliuk, the sea goddess. The missionaries say that's wrong."

Elizapee held it to her ear and was astonished at the sound she heard.

"Where did this come from?" Elizapee asked, pointing at an ornament hanging on the wall.

"That's a woman's necklace. The long front pieces are made of beads and ivory. Important women used to wear those. They were given to them by their mothers to wear at feasts and dances. But long ago, the main way for a girl to become beautiful was to have tattoos."

"Tattoos?" said Elizapee. "Uvilu told me her grandmother had tattoos."

"So have I," said Sala proudly. "Look at mine." She rolled back her left sleeve almost to the elbow. "Look at that arm tattoo. Isn't it a beauty? Girls today don't bother with tattoos. They don't care if their arms and legs don't look handsome."

Elizapee bent forward and examined Sala's arm. Her tattoos were blue and about as wide as a ballpoint pen stroke and as long as needles. Some of these tattoo marks were feathered on the ends like arrows. At her wrist, the tattooing looked like a small bracelet. Farther up on the inside of her arm was one small single mark.

"What is that?" asked Elizapee.

"*Apoutee,* snowflake," Sala answered.

Elizapee's eyes widened and her mouth flew open.

"I've got one just like that," she whispered. And pulling up the left sleeves of her parka and shirt, she showed Sala her own small blue tattoo.

Sala's old eyes narrowed as she took a tight hold on Elizapee's arm and bent very close, examining it with care.

"Well, girl," said the old woman, "you may find this hard to believe, but I put that tattoo mark on you. Yes, I'm the one who put that snowflake on your arm when you were a very young baby. You are my granddaughter. Your real name is not Elizapee. It's Apoutee!"

XVI

"ARE YOU SURE?" ELIZAPEE STARED INTO THE OLD woman's eyes.

"Of course I'm sure," said Sala. "We've been looking for you, asking for you, wondering how to find you all these years."

"Well, then, you must know—" Elizapee stopped, for she could hardly breathe or speak. "What about—my—mother and my father?"

The old woman smiled and patted Elizapee's hand. "Your father's the one who built this high house for me. His name is Namoni. And your mother—she's working, selling long winter underwear not far away from here over at the Hudson's Bay Company store. You could go and see her. Her name is Mukitu. Everyone knows her over there."

"Oh, thank you, I've got to go now," said Elizapee in a trembling voice. "May I come back to see you later?"

"Of course you can. You're my granddaughter."

Sala helped rope Elizapee down the stairs. Uvilu was waiting to catch her.

"Can you believe—I'm Sala's granddaughter! Hurry! Follow me!" Elizapee said. Together they ran to the red-roofed Hudson's Bay Company store, which was not too far away.

To the first person who seemed to be a clerk in the store, Elizapee gasped, "Do you know someone working here named Mukitu?"

"*Ajii.*" The woman smiled. "Mukitu is right over there, selling that man some long winter underwear."

"Thank you," said Elizapee, and she and Uvilu hurried across the store.

The woman turned and looked at the two girls strangely, then turned back to her customer.

He said in Inuktitut, "*Kenowya katchinik?*"

Elizapee heard her new-found mother tell him the price. Then she took him to the checkout counter.

"Can I help you, girls?" her mother asked when she returned.

"You're . . . You are Mukitu?" Elizapee asked in a shaking voice.

"Yes, I am Mukitu."

"Mukitu, I believe I am your daughter, Apoutee," Elizapee said, using her true name for the first time.

Her mother stepped back stiffly, her eyes wide with surprise. "How could you be? How do you know that? You've been lost for so many years. Where have you been?"

"First I was in the hospital, then school in the south. I've been looking everywhere to find you," Elizapee cried. "Here, look at my arm." She pulled up her left sleeve and showed her mother the small tattoo of the snowflake. "I just saw my grandmother, Sala. She said she put that mark on me."

"I remember her doing it down at our camp," said Mukitu breathlessly. "You were just a baby in my hood!"

Her mother reached out, shook hands with her daughter, as she should, then with Uvilu. There was a nervous silence among them.

"Where is my father, Namoni?" Elizapee asked her mother.

Mukitu looked up at the store clock. "He should be working right now. He runs the government snowplow over at the airport. He keeps the runways clear." She led both girls to the window in the door and pointed. "There he is climbing up into his big yellow machine. Go right now and say hello to him. Tell him you are his lost daughter, Apoutee. Tell him kind of slowly or he might fall down!" She nodded to the two girls. "I'm busy now. I'll see you later."

Elizapee walked slowly along the snowy road beside Uvilu. Neither of them spoke at first.

"That isn't at all the way I thought our first meeting would be," said Elizapee. "I've been waiting so long for this moment to come."

"I think your mother was just surprised and nervous. Probably it won't be the same with your father. I'll bet he'll be really glad to see you. Let's go down to that gate. Hurry, so we'll be there before his snowplow passes."

They were waiting just inside the fence when the big yellow plow came toward them. Both Elizapee and Uvilu waved and the driver of the big machine slowed down, then stopped. The two girls climbed the pile of snow and hurried to him as he got down.

"Is your name Namoni?" Elizapee asked him.

When he answered, *"Ajii,"* Uvilu said, "This is your daughter, Apoutee. We call her Elizapee. She's been looking for you for a long time."

"You're fooling me!" Namoni laughed. "My daughter? We don't know where she is. We think she's dead."

"We wouldn't fool you," said Elizapee nervously. "I've just been to see my grandmother, your mother, Sala. She remembers making this small *apoutee* on my arm." Elizapee pulled up her sleeve and showed it to her father.

He looked at it, then wild-eyed at her, then formally shook hands with his daughter for the first time, and with Uvilu. "Well, this is some day! Does your mother know you're back? Have you seen her yet?"

"Yes . . . I've seen her." Elizapee nodded, then she started to cry.

"You go ahead and cry. I would," said Uvilu, putting her arm around Elizapee's trembling shoulders and handing her a big red handkerchief to dry her tears. "This is the day you've been waiting for for so long."

Elizapee's father looked sad and upset and could think of nothing more to say. He looked at his wrist-watch. "I've got to get back on the machine and finish clearing this airstrip before the afternoon plane comes in. I'll see you later over at our house around five-thirty. You must know where our house is by now."

Elizapee nodded. "I'll be there." She watched her father climb back onto the plow and move it forward, skillfully angling the snow pile off its blade, yet looking back at her.

"What can we do until five-thirty?" Elizapee asked. "We don't have anywhere to go."

"Yes, we have," said Uvilu. "The lights are on now. We're going right into that inn. They serve food, and we're each going to have a great big hamburger and a tall milk shake to celebrate you finding your family. They both kind of look like you and I'll bet they'll both turn out to be very nice parents. Don't worry. They were just sort of knocked speechless. Imagine you meeting your own almost-grown-up daughter for the first time since she was a baby riding naked in your hood."

"I feel so nervous I can hardly speak," Elizapee answered in a trembling voice.

She ate less than half her hamburger and kept glancing at the big wall clock over the kitchen door.

Just then, Tomasi and Poota came in and sat down beside them.

"Sharni went back to Apex to visit her cousins. Have you two had a good day?" Poota asked.

Uvilu looked at Elizapee and saw that she might start to cry again. Changing the subject quickly, Uvilu asked Tomasi, "Did you find your friends, Kayak and Mattoosie, in Apex?"

"No," said Tomasi. "But I saw Charlie, the Australian helicopter pilot who flies *Waltzing Matilda*. He told me Kayak and Mattoosie—whose real name is Matthew Morgan, you know—were away, visiting in San Diego, California, and going to school down there this year. They're living with a girl and her father they met up here. Her name is Jill.

"How about you, Elizapee?" Tomasi asked her. "Did you have an interesting day?"

"Yes. I found . . . my family . . . my grandmother, my mother, and my father."

"Holy smoke!" yelled Tomasi.

"*Atow!* Wonderful!" Poota shouted, and he pounded on the table. "After all your years of searching, you've finally found your family." Then he paused and sat in silence, as if he were studying the salt and pepper shakers. "Does that mean you're not going back to Nesak Island? That you're going to stay here with them? Live here in Iqaluit?"

Elizapee looked at him and swallowed hard. "*Kauyimangilunga,*" she answered. "I don't know." And then she did begin to cry.

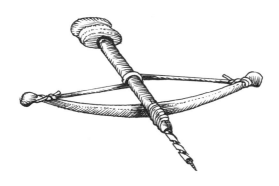

XVII

THAT EVENING, ELIZABETH QUEEN WENT AGAIN TO the house of her true family and knocked on the door. The weather seemed warm enough, so she had put on her best parka from the south and her orange-and-yellow scarf. Somehow, she had lost her feelings of being either Elizapee or Apoutee. She seemed to have gone backward into some earlier self who had just arrived up north in George's plane.

A porch light came on and her mother, Mukitu, opened the door. They smiled at each other as Elizabeth came in out of the lightly falling snow.

"Hang your parka inside," her mother said. "It's too cold to leave it in the porch."

When they entered the small, neat living room, they heard a thumping noise somewhere above.

"That's Namoni, your . . . father. He's helping your grandmother, Sala, down. She almost never visits us from that high tower of hers, but she's so excited about having found you that she wouldn't miss coming down tonight."

Mukitu pointed to the sofa and Elizabeth sat tensely while her mother went to the kitchen, then returned carrying a tray with four mugs, a pot of coffee, sugar, milk, and a box of Hudson's Bay Company cookies. They heard feet stamping off snow in the porch, and Elizabeth's father, Namoni, opened the door and guided his mother, Sala, into their living room.

"Those are clever stairs that Namoni built, and I like them," Sala said to Mukitu. "Nobody else but Namoni can climb those stairs unless I lower the rope to help them." She smiled at Elizabeth. "When I wish to come down, your father comes and helps me.

"It must be strange for you, dear Apoutee, all of a sudden finding your father, mother, and grandmother," said Sala. "Oh, yes, and you've got an older brother and two older sisters, but none of them lives here. They're scattered north and west."

"Tell us about yourself," Elizabeth's father said. "What happened to you after you were taken away on that ship?"

"Oh, we felt so bad!" her mother said.

Elizabeth told them all that she could first remember and how, for the past year, she had been searching for them in many settlements and camps.

"When you came through here looking for us, we were probably living north at Pangnirtung," her father said. "Well, we're all together now." He began to tell Elizabeth which camps and settlements they'd lived in since their parting long ago.

"You can stay on here and go to school," her mother

told her. "You're tall for your age. Next year, I might be able to get you a job sweeping up at the Company store and later, maybe, you could learn to be a clerk."

Elizabeth did not answer.

"Do you want to stay here?" her father asked.

"I . . . I don't know," Elizabeth answered. "It's wonderful to have found you and to know who I am at last. But I had been hoping that you would be living in a place like, maybe, Nesak Island, or at our fish camp on the Kokjuak."

"You've got good ideas," her grandmother said. "I wish I still camped out on the land the way we did before."

"Well, we can't do that anymore," said her mother firmly. "I've got a good job here with the Company, and your father works for the government. He's known to be the best snow mover anywhere around here. Nobody from the south can move snow or stand the winter winds like your father can."

"Still, being here is not at all like living in the camps," said Sala, "being close to your best friends and all the animals. Being able to pick up and go anytime you set your mind to it."

"I know what you mean," Elizabeth said. "And I'm just starting to learn my own language again."

"You're getting good at it," her father remarked. "More Inuit kids use English around here every day, it seems."

"They don't use English much on Nesak Island, except when Tomasi is there teaching. So it's much easier for me to learn the language out there. I really like the Kiawak family. They have helped me so much."

"We know them just a bit," her mother said. "They are good people. If you wanted to go back out to live with them, we wouldn't mind." Mukitu looked at her husband and his mother, Sala.

"I think she should go back," said Sala. "I think she'd be lucky to go back. I envy her! Good night, Apoutee." Her grandmother looked sad. She stood up and her son helped her to get back up into her tower.

"It's getting late," said Elizabeth's mother, and she pulled out the sofa-chair that unfolded into a narrow bed. "If you need anything, just ask me for it. It's been so long that we have been apart that it's hard for me to start to think again that we are mother and daughter. Perhaps it will be different when I see you next time. Good night, Apoutee."

Elizabeth could hear her father in the tower with her grandmother. They were still talking when Elizabeth, exhausted from so many good, yet strange, happenings in a single day, fell sound asleep.

She woke early in the morning. It was dark outside and her parents were still in their bedroom. The house creaked in the cold. She got up, went quietly to the bathroom, and dressed. Then she smoothed and folded the sheets and blanket, and closed the chair-bed. She pulled on her boots, scarf, and parka, and went outside.

Uvilu had been right. Her pale-blue parka with no fur trim was far too thin for this wintry weather. She bound her scarf around her head and neck, pulled up her hood, and hurried along the long snow road that led to Apex, where the Kiawak family was staying.

She had not gone far when a police car pulled up beside her. It had red lights on and ROYAL CANADIAN MOUNTED POLICE, NWT and a buffalo-head crest painted on its door.

The door beside her opened and a young police officer leaned over and said, "*Bonjour, mademoiselle.* You're out early. May I give you a lift?"

"*Oui, merci. Il fait froid,*" said Elizabeth Queen, pleased to be able to answer him in French. She got in beside him. He wore no outer coat, and the car seemed boiling hot.

"Where would you like to go?"

"To that blue house with all the new snowmobiles out in front," said Elizabeth. "I'm with the Kiawak family. They've been able to buy those with money they earned from their carvings."

"Oh, yes, they just arrived in town. Kiawak's known to be one of the best carvers in the Arctic, everyone says." The police officer added, "Your English is really good. Have you always lived in that camp? Are you one of Tomasi's students?"

"Yes, I am, but I haven't always lived with the Nesak Island people."

They sat together for five minutes in the police car outside the blue house while she told him about her strange life and the finding of her family yesterday.

"There are lots of good people living here," the officer told her. "Folks would welcome you, if you stay. Everyone likes your mom and dad."

"I like them, too," said Elizabeth. "But . . . Well

. . . Right now, I don't know what to do. I really want to live out in the camp at Nesak."

"If I can be of any help, Elizabeth, you let me know," said the young police officer in French as Elizabeth got out.

"*Merci encore*," she said, closing the car door. She hurried into the blue house.

Uvilu was sitting by herself in the morning silence, drinking a cup of tea. "I've been waiting for you to come back here. Now tell me everything that's happened. What are you going to do?"

"I don't know." Elizabeth sighed as she pulled off her parka. "It's really hard for me to know what's best."

"It must be," Uvilu agreed. "Your friend and ours, George Charity, the pilot, came here last night and ate some caribou with us. He said he's got to make two flights over our way and he'll gladly fly you, too, Elizapee, if you want to come back to Nesak Island with us. But everyone's afraid to ask you because you just found your own real family here.

"My father and Tudlik are giving George four really good stone carvings in exchange for the plane ride," said Uvilu. "It's up to you. But you're welcome to come with us. I mean, we've all grown sort of used to you—Poota, Tomasi, Sharni, me, my grandfather, my mother and father, everybody. Sharni told me she likes you."

"I'm going to sit here and think about everything," Elizabeth told Uvilu. "Then I'll talk to your family when they get up."

Later that morning, no one said, "Oh, you should

come with us," or "You should stay here with your new-found family." Nobody said anything really, but they all gave Elizabeth their kindest looks.

"Will you come with me and see my family?" Elizabeth finally asked them. "They'll be home as soon as they're finished work at half past five."

"Yes, we will," said Kiawak and Maylee. "We'll all go see them, this whole family."

And they did. The porch light was on to welcome them. Elizabeth's father was just bringing her grandmother, Sala, down into their lower house. Elizabeth's mother had tea and biscuits ready for everyone.

"Mukitu, I haven't seen you since we were *uvikait*, teenagers," Maylee said to Elizabeth's mother. "We don't come to this big airport place very often."

When the visiting was almost ended, Kiawak said, "If the weather's good, we'll be flying back to Nesak Island tomorrow morning."

"Lucky you!" the grandmother said.

There was a silence in the hot, crowded room.

Elizabeth sat forward. "I am thrilled to have found you, my family. But I have just started to become Inuk again, to learn the language and the way camp people move and live. I love it at Nesak Island and I want to go on living in that way. Maylee, Kiawak, all the people in the camp say I'm welcome to go back and live with them. It's what I want to do."

Elizabeth's mother and father were silent.

Her grandmother, Sala, said, "Apoutee, you go and do it! I wish I were young like you."

"Why don't you come with Elizapee," said Kiawak, "and visit us for the winter?"

"We need a nice grandmother like you," Maylee told her. "There's room for you in the airplane."

"Go, if you want to go, you two," Elizabeth's mother said to both the grandmother and Elizabeth. "Namoni and I can't go. We both have our jobs here."

"You two do just what you want to do," Elizabeth's father said to his mother and to his daughter whom he had never really known.

"This will be my last chance to live the good country life again." Sala's eyes brightened. "If these Nesak Islanders are willing to take me, I'm going to go with Apoutee, or maybe I'll start calling her Elizapee, the way these others do."

"I'm going to sleep here in my family's house again tonight," Elizabeth told them, "but my grandmother and I will both be ready to go with you tomorrow."

"Oh, I'm glad!" said Poota, who had been very quiet during the whole visit.

"*Uvungalu.* Me, too," said everyone in the Kiawak family. "Now we've got to go and get some sleep before our journey home."

XVIII

BY MIDMORNING ON THE FOLLOWING DAY, THE SKY
had brightened, but the weather was stinging cold.
The early winter sun scarcely rose above the hills and
traveled sideways, as though it could hardly wait to
climb back into bed.

George, the pilot, had had his sturdy, bright-red
plane towed out of the warm hangar and onto the
runway. He was revving up the engine for the flight.
Elizapee, Poota, and Uvilu already stood beside the
plane and watched Kiawak, with Maylee, bringing
Elizapee's grandmother, Sala, out to the plane on his
new blue snowmobile fully paid for by his carvings.
Namoni, Elizapee's father, saw them coming. He shut
off the engine of his government snowplow and, climbing down, he hurried toward the plane. His wife,
Mukitu, arrived a few moments later, jumping out of
a small truck. She carried two bright packages. Now,

suddenly, they were all together. George opened the rear cargo door and he and Poota started stuffing in the baggage.

"I like the way Inuit travel light." George laughed. "Looks like you are all going away for a weekend instead of nearly a year."

"Don't forget," said Poota, "you are bringing us another planeload of the things we ordered. And Tudlik, Nuna, and Sharni are going to bring our new snowmobiles over to the island as soon as Tudlik thinks the snow and ice are solid. Tomasi will come then, too, and do the teaching."

"That won't be very long," said Sala, sniffing the wind. "I can almost smell real snow coming through the air." She shuffled her feet and said to Uvilu, "You ask the *tingmijurtit*, pilot, when we are going to go. I've never been up in one of these tin birds. Tell him to get going quick before someone decides that I'm too old to fly."

Uvilu translated for George, who smiled at the old woman and said, "Lady, we're going now! You can sit up in front with me and see all the sights."

"*Tavvauvusit ilunasi*, good-bye, everyone," Elizapee's father and mother called, and they hugged or shook hands with everyone climbing into the plane.

"Oh, I almost forgot these presents," said Mukitu, leaning inside. "They're from both of us to you, Elizapee Apoutee, and to you, Sala. Good long winter underwear from my department in the Company's store." She ducked out of the plane.

Hugo slammed the rear door and waved good-bye

to the passengers. It was going to be a short flight and the engine had just been checked, so to let old Sala have the front seat, he and George had decided Hugo should remain behind.

The plane's single engine roared as it gathered increasing speed and took off smoothly over the cold, blue bay. Beyond them they could see ridge after ridge of mountains fading into the distant Arctic haze.

Some time passed before Sala pointed out the windshield, then called back to Elizapee, "There it is, the shining glacier. They call her Silveea. Our old camp is down there near the edge, right by that little river. It's the place where I was born, where your parents, and you, Elizapee Apoutee, were born."

Elizapee stared hard out of her window as George winged the plane down low beside the frozen river and the ancient stone rings that marked her first home. When Elizapee turned to look at her grandmother, Sala was still staring back at her. Their eyes filled with tears, not tears of sadness, but of joy.

Now the plane soared high again and flew straight across the curving spines of mountains until Kiawak pointed down and they could all see the deep fjord where they had left the white boat. Yes, it was there. They could see hunters, women, and children scattering, running on the snow, waving up to them. They hoped that old Paar, the grandfather, who had stayed with his married daughter to avoid the long, cold ride to Frobisher Bay, was still safe and well. Other adults from Nesak had stayed behind for the same reason. The trip on the snowmobiles was for younger people.

The plane rose higher and flew along the coast.

Elizapee felt a warm hand on her shoulder. "There it is!" Poota told her. "You can just see it in the haze. It's our island. We're almost home."

"It does look like your hat from up here." Elizapee smiled at him. "It feels so wonderful to be coming home again."

As the plane lowered and began to circle, they could see into the island's one small bay.

"There are snowmobile tracks. Who made them?" Uvilu called out. "How did they get there?"

"Can't you see the footprints? Someone was walking ahead, testing the strength of the ice. That's the way your grandfather usually does things," Maylee said. "I was sure he would want to get back here before we arrived. He must have talked his daughter's husband and some other young hunter from that camp into bringing over the older people who stayed behind."

"Your grandfather," Kiawak told Poota, "doesn't like to miss a thing. And it's my guess that he brought all our winter clothing and those boxes filled with carvings."

As the plane dipped even lower, Uvilu could see her grandfather hurrying stiff-legged across the snow with Lao beside him. Two younger men were standing waving up at them.

"Look at that!" said George. "Old Paar's got two wind socks hanging out on the ice in front of the island to show me which way the wind is blowing and where the drifts are not too rough for landing."

Sala laughed when Elizapee interpreted the pilot's

words for her. "You tell him," said Sala, "you don't get old for nothing. Sometimes some old folks even get a little wiser."

George completed his circle around Nesak Island and came in low between the two wind socks, which were somebody's old blue jeans, blowing like a pair of eager sprinters galloping sideways on the north wind. It was not what most people would call a nice smooth landing, but it was the best that could be done in such a place. Down on the ice, everything was in blue shadow now, for the sun had disappeared behind the hills.

Uvilu said to George, "My mother asks you to come up with us to say hello to my grandfather and have some tea."

George smiled and wiped the frost off his glasses. "You tell your mother and all the others thanks. But I've got to go again right now before this engine cools. I'm flying straight to Cape Dorset to check in with my Frobisher base. When I return with your supplies and pick up your carvings for the Dorset Co-op, I'll visit with you then. So, good-bye and good luck to all of you, and especially you, Elizabeth Queen. You really have found two wonderful families and a home at last."

"My thanks to you, George." Elizapee hugged him. "Thank my friends down south, too, and tell them that I'm happier now than I've been in all my life."

As the plane took off, they walked up over the snow-covered beach toward their friends who had returned to the island. They greeted each other warmly, glad to see again those from the Pudlo and Kakak families.

Three of the four big, double-walled winter tents were already standing.

"Some good place!" said Sala as she stopped in front of the Kiawak family tent, which was carefully snow-blocked and rounded on all corners against the wildness of the winds. She turned, looking all around. "Some wonderful island for us to spend a winter."

"Winters are the best time here," said Uvilu. "You wait until you hear my grandfather tell his stories. He's got one about bears that will make you want to jump out of your skin!"

Uvilu's grandfather laughed and looked at Sala with pleasure in his eyes.

"I can hardly wait," said Sala. "I've got a few stories to tell all of you myself. Some, I hope, you've never heard."

"It's really cold out here," Elizapee said, for she was still wearing her light-blue parka and shivering. "Maybe I should go inside."

"Don't you be too quick, granddaughter," she said, throwing her woolen shawl around Elizapee's shoulders. "I have a very old song to sing before I place my foot inside an important winter home like this."

"What is the song?" everyone asked.

Sala turned twice around and sang out the ancient words that were perhaps as old as the time when humans had first dared to follow this farthest northern trail around the earth. Then she sang to them strongly, for she wanted everyone to hear—perhaps even the spirits of the ancient people from the past and other new ones from the future who had not yet been born.

"Glorious it is
when wandering time
has come.
Glorious it is
to see the changing lands,
the changing seasons.
Glorious it is
to be alive."

Elizapee Apoutee closed her eyes and tried to hold each word of Sala's song inside herself forever.

When Elizapee opened her eyes, all the others had gone inside their tents, except Poota. He stood silently in the twilight, waiting for her. Elizapee looked at him and at the snowflakes falling down. She felt a warmth come over her as she spread her arms and called up to the night sky:

"Drifting snow,
why do I sing?"